Enemies of Medicine Feather

Few white men know the land west of the Missouri like Weston Gray, renowned hunter, tracker and guide. The Arapaho and Lakota Sioux people with whom he has lived from time to time call him Medicine Feather, and he has acted as interpreter and spokesman for them so they avoid trouble with the military, and at treaty meetings with Washington delegates. Among the people he calls 'friend' are army officers and tribal chieftains, who listen to his advice in order to maintain peace. But the discovery of gold in the Black Hills has changed the mood on both sides, and now, in the summer of 1876, Wes no longer knows if he has any friends along the frontier. He does know that he has enemies.

By the same author

The Hanging of Charlie Darke
The Drummond Brand
In the High Bitterroots
Return to Tatanka Crossing
A Storm in Montana
Longhorn Justice
Medicine Feather
Arkansas Bushwhackers
Jefferson's Saddle
Along the Tonto Rim
The Gambler and the Law
Lakota Justice
Crackaway's Quest
Riding the Line
To the Far Sierras
Black Hills Gold
Feud along the Dearborn
Remarque's Law
Red Diamond Rustlers
Ridgeway's Bride

Enemies of Medicine Feather

Will DuRey

A Black Horse Western

ROBERT HALE

© Will DuRey 2020
First published in Great Britain 2020

ISBN 978-0-7198-3085-3

The Crowood Press
The Stable Block
Crowood Lane
Ramsbury
Marlborough
Wiltshire SN8 2HR

www.bhwesterns.com

Robert Hale is an imprint
of The Crowood Press

The right of Will DuRey to be identified as
author of this work has been asserted by him
in accordance with the Copyright, Designs and
Patents Act 1988

All rights reserved. No part of this publication may be
reproduced or transmitted in any form or by any means,
electronic or mechanical, including photocopying, recording,
or any information storage and retrieval system, without
permission in writing from the publishers.

Typeset by
Derek Doyle & Associates, Shaw Heath
Printed and bound in Great Britain by
4Bind Ltd, Stevenage, SG1 2XT

ONE

Instinct alone drew Wes Gray to the small copse on the knoll. Nothing distinguished it from any of the other groves he'd passed, of which there were countless in these vast, wide-open spaces of the western plains. The movement of neither game nor bird had caught his attention, no guttural grunt of a grazing buck or screech of a searching bird of prey had directed his eyes in that direction, but ever since he'd ridden within its proximity his attention had been fixed on it. The half-dozen trees, neither too small nor too large to warrant interest, leant in his direction, twisted by their long defiance of those wild winds that sometimes swept the hillsides. Yet it was something in the way their topmost boughs were tipped that beckoned him, like a military burial party, heads bowed in sadness or shame.

Wes was yet fifty yards distant when he halted, pausing long enough to absorb his surroundings. Although a hint of smoke could be detected on the northern breeze he knew its source was neither close nor threatening. In fact he was certain that he was not in any physical danger. Still, before urging his horse steadily forwards, he withdrew his rifle from its sheath and rested the stock on his right thigh. The dappled filly Wes was riding seemed to tremble as it approached the trees, as though his caution had spooked it.

Five bodies were strewn in the long grass, three men and two horses. Although bullet holes were clear to see on the stripped bodies, they were also pierced by a multitude of arrows. Death had been dealt viciously to these men. They had been scalped, and hatchet blows had disfigured their features.

Again, Wes Gray remained motionless until he was certain that another attack was not imminent. The prints of four or five unshod ponies scuffed the ground. They were recent marks, perhaps less than an hour old, and they told their own story. The killers had fled this place and were riding hard to escape discovery. They wouldn't return any time soon.

Wes dismounted and looked at each of the dead men, but it was impossible to tell if any of them had been known to him. He looked at the arrows and knew from their markings that the attack had been carried out by warriors of the Ogallalah Sioux, a conclusion that gave him additional cause for concern. His wife's people were Ogallalah, and although Apo Hopa now lived in his house on the V-shaped piece of land where the Mildwater Creek meets the South

Platte River, her father and brother still lived in a nearby village. In recent years, under the leadership of Chief Red Knife, few disputes had arisen between that group and the soldiers of Fort Hamilton. They'd watched each other warily, but no battles or skirmishes had occurred to occasion injuries, deaths or resentments. The Sioux had pursued their own lifestyle without hindrance, while the soldiers' fort had become a place to trade goods and customs.

But this year, the mood of the Plains tribes had become belligerent, the demands and threats from Washington having re-awakened the tension that eight years earlier had culminated in Red Cloud's War. Now, because gold had been found in the Black Hills, the government had chosen to rip up the resulting Laramie Treaty. The people of the Sioux, Cheyenne and Arapaho nations were to be confined to agencies, which would effectively terminate the nomadic lifestyle of these hunter people. Since the end of the Civil War, to encourage the settlement of the West, the policy of confining the tribes-people had grown in popularity. Settlers and ranching magnates wanted the land, and argued that those already there needed to learn new ways, or perish. On agency land, it was argued, they would acquire the skill to support themselves through agriculture. But farming was a foreign concept to the proud tribesmen, and many voices were raised against the government's new demands. They would rather fight and die than submit to the military's restrictions.

ENEMIES OF MEDICINE FEATHER

Wes Gray had long known that the way of life of the Lakota people and their allies was threatened by the rapid advancement of American civilization. The railroads across the prairie had led to the slaughter of the great buffalo herds, the millions that had roamed the plains reduced in a handful of years to a seldom seen few. They had been the mainstay of life for the tribes-people, every part of their body necessary for the provision of food, clothing, weapons and tools. He wasn't alone in acknowledging that change was inevitable. The wise men of the nations knew it too, and they knew that the white men were countless, that they were able to replace every man they lost in battle with ten more.

Even so, the warriors were prepared to fight again because they were finally aware that the promises from Washington were worthless. As part of the 1868 Treaty of Laramie, lines had been drawn on maps that designated the boundaries of the Great Sioux Reservation, within which white men were not allowed to settle, and beyond which the Sioux would not raid. But the Black Hills, the holy area of the Paha Sapa, were part of that reservation, and persuaded by rumours of gold, the government had ordered an expedition into the Black Hills without first informing the Sioux. This insult had been seriously magnified when the identity of the expedition leader became known: Custer. Custer had attacked the sleeping village of peaceful Southern Cheyenne along the Washita, and was despised by all the tribesmen of the

ENEMIES OF MEDICINE FEATHER

Plains. There would never be forgiveness for the man who had ordered the slaughter of men, women and children that morning. Even though the American flag flew outside the tepee of their chief, Black Kettle, Custer had ordered the destruction of every home and had hounded the survivors across the frozen landscape.

It was Wes Gray's opinion that Custer's verdict on the expedition to the Black Hills had been deliberately inciting. 'Gold from the grass roots down,' he'd proclaimed, instigating an unchecked stampede of prospectors onto the Reservation land that had, inevitably, aroused the wrath of the tribes. They called the route travelled by the gold-seekers the 'Thieves' Road', and described Custer as the 'Chief of Thieves'. To protect the sacred Paha Sapa, many of the miners who came in search of *mazaska zi*, yellow metal, were killed.

Paltry attempts to purchase the Black Hills from the Sioux were attempted by the government, but eventually President Grant was persuaded to abandon negotiations. Instead, he instructed the confinement of the people of the Plains tribes to the newly established agencies. In February, the War Department ordered General Sheridan to regard as hostile any of those Sioux, Cheyenne and Arapaho people who hadn't yet concurred with the government's edict. This year, 1876, the centennial year of the founding of the United States of America, they planned to sweep away forever the free-roaming

ENEMIES OF MEDICINE FEATHER

lifestyle of the tribes of the Plains.

Although the dead men were naked, Wes had no doubt that they had been serving members of the cavalry. Bloodied though their bodies were, their facial hair, sideburns and moustaches were in trim order, indicative of military discipline. In addition, he could clearly see the brand of the US Cavalry burned into the rump of one of the dead horses. He would have to carry the news of the killings to Fort Hamilton. Whatever their mission, the commanding officer would want to know that it had come to an abrupt end – but Wes hesitated before remounting and heading in that direction.

As had been his practice for the past ten years, Wes had signed up to act as Caleb Dodge's chief scout for the wagon train he was leading to California. Despite the rumours of possible conflict between the army and the tribes, it had been Caleb's opinion that any fighting would take place far to the north of the recognized wagon route. Wes had agreed. The absence of buffalo meant that the best hunting grounds were situated in the Yellowstone and Powder River country. Still, he'd decided to ride ahead of the wagons and gather the latest information from Fort Hamilton. It would be four or five days before the wagons caught up with him, which meant that first he had time to visit his wife, Apo Hopa.

Fort Hamilton was five miles west of this place, while his home on the Mildwater Creek was a similar distance to the north. He was reluctant to abandon the plan that would get him back to Fort Hamilton in time to meet up with the westward-bound wagons. There was nothing he could do for the dead men. They weren't going anywhere. Then something caught his eye which put a new slant on his deliberations.

He'd glanced at the dead horses when he'd first entered the grove, had identified them both as cavalry animals, and had decided that the third horse, if uninjured, had been taken by the fleeing warriors. But now, as he sat astride his dappled filly, he noted that the harness on one of the dead horses was not standard cavalry equipment. Furthermore, the saddle was one designed for a woman.

From the top of the knoll he scanned all around, looking for any area of disturbed grass where another body might lie. There was nothing, only the line caused by the fleeing warriors that marked their trail north-west to the low hills. They had a prisoner, a prize to take back to their village, a slave who would be abused and used for every menial task. Wes considered chasing them in the hope of securing her release, but soon abandoned that idea. The warriors were riding towards Red Knife's village, which indicated that a welcome awaited them there. That could only mean that this wasn't an isolated incident, that open hostilities existed between the soldiers and the Sioux, and even though he had hereto been acknowledged as friend of the tribes-people, there were still those who regarded him with suspicion. Until he was aware of all the facts he would avoid contact with them.

An hour later he reached Fort Hamilton. The first thing he noticed was that the usual collection of tepees around the entrance gates was much reduced, and most of those remaining had been abandoned. Those Cheyenne, Sioux and Arapaho people who had found a niche acting as interpreters, go-betweens and traders, had gone. The second thing that struck him as odd was the way a couple of old regular soldiers refused to look his way as he rode across the parade ground. He wasn't a stranger to this place, and on several occasions had been hired as a guide for an expedition or as translator at a parlay. His knowledge and skills were legendary, his advice often sought on Indian affairs.

He hitched his horse outside the long building, part of which was the office of the commanding officer. Colonel Finch said it was good to see him again, but there was no smile of welcome, merely wariness in his eyes. It seemed to Wes that the colonel had been expecting him, and expecting trouble to come with the visit. If that was the case, Wes wasn't about to disappoint him.

'I found three dead soldiers east of here,' he said. 'Stripped and with enough arrows in them to kill them ten times over.'

'You're sure they were soldiers?'

'Two dead animals bearing your brand.'

'East of here, you say. None of my patrols are in that area.'

ENEMIES OF MEDICINE FEATHER

Again, Wes was left with the impression that the words had been uttered to hide the colonel's true thoughts. 'Probably wasn't a patrol,' he said. 'There was a woman with them.'

'A woman!' exclaimed the colonel, then as though spurred by a sudden, dreadful thought, he shouted for the sergeant at work in the outer office. 'Where's Miss Goodwin?'

'She went riding, sir, with Lieutenants Clarke, Harte and Anderson.'

'How long have they been gone?'

'Three hours, sir.' He paused, directed a look at Wes Gray before adding, 'I believe they were planning a picnic, sir. The young lady wanted to see the village.'

'Red Knife's village?' asked Wes Gray.

Colonel Finch had a stony face when he nodded his response, his lips pressed tightly together as though afraid that too many words would escape if he opened them.

'Then I guess she's got her wish,' Wes announced, 'because the raiding party took her with them.'

Colonel Finch had been in command at Fort Hamilton for several years – he was an experienced officer, cool under pressure, quick to assess situations in accordance with military procedure. But now he seemed to be struggling to make a decision. 'We must get her back,' he said at last. 'Wes, we'll need your help.'

'You need to tell me why Red Knife's braves are

killing soldiers.'

'You know Washington's edict,' the colonel replied. 'Everyone had to go to an agency by the end of February.'

'A ridiculous order. Most people were still in their winter settlements then, they couldn't have crossed the plains in those conditions even if they'd chosen to obey.'

'Not obeying classified them as hostile.'

'Red Knife and his people weren't hostile,' retorted Wes. 'They would need to hunt, provide themselves with food before making such a trek.'

'They were told that food would be provided at the agency,' Colonel Finch told him.

'They're proud people. They would want to travel with dignity, not like paupers. Didn't you tell that to your superiors?'

Colonel Finch objected to Wes Gray's manner. 'I did what I could,' he answered, 'but I'm a soldier and had orders to obey. Time had run out for them. It was necessary for them to move.'

'So what have you done?'

'I haven't done anything but re-supply the troop under Captain Faraday's command. They arrived under special orders to escort all tribes-people to the Red Cloud Agency.'

Although the soldier's words were meant to deflect Wes's criticism, they merely heightened his concern. If a special company had been raised to compel the tribes-people to leave their homes, it would be done mercilessly. Without prior contact with the Sioux the mission would be carried out without care or pity for those in their charge. If the army followed its past policy, then the people of Red Knife's village would have been stripped not only of arms, but horses, too. Men, women and children, the sick and feeble, would be forced to walk to Red Cloud's Agency, and that was a trek of more than two hundred miles.

'When did they leave?' Wes wanted to know.

'Four days ago,' he was told. 'But Wes,' added Colonel Finch, 'we must rescue Annabelle Goodwin. She's a visitor, a friend of Captain Littlefair's daughter, but her reason for being here was to meet her brother, who is a First Lieutenant under Captain Faraday's command.'

'And she was eager to see the destruction that he and his well-armed soldiers were capable of inflicting on a peaceful village.'

'Of course not, Wes.' Then, with a voice less full of conviction, he added, 'We don't even know that damage was done to those people or their property.'

'I could smell the smoke more than five miles away,' Wes told him, 'and what other reason would prompt the braves to attack your young officers?'

'Then it was done in accordance with orders issued by a higher authority than mine,' Colonel Finch told him. 'You know I've worked for peace with the Sioux ever since I arrived here. I like Red Knife and several of the other chiefs.'

ENEMIES OF MEDICINE FEATHER

'But orders are orders, is that right, Colonel?'

'Yes. That's right. If Red Knife had taken his people to the agency as instructed, then it wouldn't have been necessary to enforce the order by putting troops in the field.'

'So now you've got a fight on your hands.'

'A fight!'

'I reckon it's what Washington has been seeking ever since Red Cloud won his war in '68, and no doubt this time the army will win, but it won't be without casualties. I need to get back to the wagons to prepare the pilgrims for possible attacks.'

'The girl, Wes. I need your help to find her.'

'There are more than three hundred people depending on me and Caleb Dodge to get them safely to California. I'm being paid to protect them, and even if it wasn't a lost cause, I'm not putting them at risk for the sake of one girl.'

'A lost cause! Do you think she's dead?'

'Possibly, but even if she's alive there's no guarantee that I could get her away from those who've captured her.'

'But they trust you, Wes. You're almost one of them.'

'Almost isn't likely to be good enough. I don't know who has her, or whether they would allow me to get close enough to parlay. A war has begun where both sides will have people who'll judge friend or enemy by the colour of a man's skin. I can't help you.'

'Wes,' the colonel was close to pleading with the scout, 'the girl's safety is vital. Her father is an important man. I think you know him. Senator Goodwin.'

TWO

Tommy O'Hara had been an early enlistment at the outbreak of the War Between the States, and now, fifteen years later, almost half his life had been spent in the army. He'd been posted west in 1870, had been one of those involved in the construction of Fort Hamilton, had been among the first troops to patrol the boundary of the newly designated reservation land, and had ridden escort for the many wagon trains that used the nearby western trails. He was a good soldier who'd risen to the rank of sergeant. He'd known Wes Gray for several years and was waiting for the scout when he left the Colonel's office.

No words were exchanged initially as Wes untied the dappled filly and led her across the parade ground to a water trough. His thunderous expression didn't invite companionship, but while he waited for the horse to drink its fill of cool water, Tommy O'Hara spoke to him.

'Bad business, Wes,' he began, 'but don't blame Colonel Finch. He's been urging Red Knife to move his people for many weeks. Told him to make his way to the Red Cloud Agency as quickly as possible, but the chief delayed and delayed until it was too late. First he said they needed to hunt to build up supplies, then their herd needed to be nourished to undertake the long journey, and then he insisted that the women needed time to prepare the pelts for clothing.'

Wes threw a sidelong glance at the sergeant, conveying the message that they were genuine needs, not tactics designed to thwart the government.

Sergeant O'Hara waved aside the scout's unspoken interruption. 'Trouble is, Wes, that a lot of Red Knife's fighting men had already left the village. My guess is that they've gone north to join Crazy Horse's Ogallalah war party. I don't doubt that they'd gone against their chief's wishes, but I guess his plan was to keep a place of refuge for them if things went bad in the Powder River country.'

Wes Gray understood the implication in the sergeant's words, knew that if Red Knife gave aid or protection to warriors who fought against the army he would be condemning the whole village to the category of hostile. But Red Knife, he knew, would not act so recklessly. Clearly he had opted to do all he could to protect his people from the ravages of war, and that those who had chosen to leave the village to fight alongside Crazy Horse would have chosen a new leader before leaving the village. But those who remained with Red Knife would include the old and infirm, and to ensure their survival along the trail to the Red Cloud Agency it would be essential to be well prepared before their trek could be undertaken. Food, clothing, and horses re-invigorated following the hardships of winter, were essential needs.

Although words of argument were forming in his mind, Wes Gray knew only too well that to utter them would achieve nothing. Perhaps Colonel Finch had striven to do right by Red Knife's people, and perhaps Sergeant O'Hara did understand that the Sioux were merely seeking to follow the mores of their ancestors, that if left undisturbed they were as eager to live in peace as most of the west-bound settlers. Perhaps, too, that was a view shared by many who already lived beyond the Missouri – but their combined voices caused little more than a whisper in Washington's debating chambers where conformity was deemed desirable, especially if it gilded the pockets of the decision makers.

Gold in the Black Hills had brought about the current threat of conflict, the discovery of which, two years earlier, had occasioned the meeting between Wes and Jeremiah Goodwin. The senator had been a member of a Washington delegation whose mission had been to renegotiate the Laramie Treaty in order to give miners access to the Black Hills. An attack on their riverboat by white men disguised as Sioux warriors had been foiled by Wes, but only later did he learn that Senator Goodwin and his son-in-law Mark Owenfield had been conspirators in the scheme. If it had succeeded, if members of the delegation had been killed by 'Sioux' warriors, Washington would have ordered the army to sweep the Indians from the hills forever. Wes's actions had avoided that outcome – but only temporarily. A conflict had been brewing ever since, and now appeared to be inevitable.

A slow-moving wagon rattled to a halt beside Wes and O'Hara. There were two soldiers on the seat and another two mounted behind.

'What do you want?' O'Hara asked the corporal sitting beside the driver.

'We're going out to collect the bodies of Lieutenants Clarke, Hart and Anderson, Sarge. Wondered if Mr Gray would act as guide.'

'I'm not going that way.'

'There's a lot of country out there. We don't want to be searching for them until it's too dark to see anything.'

'Find my trail and follow it for five miles. You'll find them in a likely picnic place.'

'Wouldn't have to look for them at all if it wasn't for your filthy killer friends,' muttered the driver.

Tommy O'Hara knew Wes Gray's black mood, and sought to put an end to the trooper's goading before the situation got out of hand. 'That's enough of that, Jackson,' he snapped.

'Good officers have been slaughtered, Sergeant, and who knows what they've done to Miss Goodwin.'

'That's enough,' repeated O'Hara.

Trooper Jackson persisted. 'It won't be enough until every one of those butchers has been killed.'

O'Hara saw the fire glowing in Wes Gray's eyes. Jackson, too wrapped up in his own certitude, did not. Surrounded by military comrades, the prospect of a violent response to the views he aired was given no consideration.

'Every one of them,' he emphasized, and sparing a surly look for Wes Gray, added, 'and that includes that squaw you keep, too.'

It was difficult to determine if Sergeant O'Hara's yell was the result of outrage at the private's remark or meant as a warning to him, but in either case it didn't save him from the consequences. Until now, it appeared to everyone that Wes Gray was only concerned with watering his horse, but at the trooper's words he sprang at the wagon with the speed, agility and suddenness of a mountain lion. Reaching across the corporal, he grabbed Jackson's tunic and dragged him from his seat.

Jerked off balance, the soldier tumbled forwards, reins falling from his grasp, arms and legs flailing as he struck the rump of one of the rear horses. It snorted, and shuffled in surprise, unsettling the other three in the team. Barged by the unseated body of his companion, the corporal gave voice to a shout of protest, but quickly stifled it when a need to calm the horses became apparent. He picked up the loose reins and called out calming words to quieten the anxious animals.

Jackson's body thumped heavily on to the ground and Wes Gray was instantly upon him. He hauled the soldier halfway to a standing position before thundering his right fist into the man's body. The blow struck Jackson just below the heart, and he sank to his knees with all the air driven from his body. Not allowing him the chance to recover, Wes threw his fist again, connecting this time with the trooper's jaw. His senses scrambled, Jackson's legs buckled and he fell against the water trough, then rolled between the legs of Wes Gray's dappled filly.

By this time, men were converging on the scene, eager to see a fight regardless of the identity of the combatants. Tommy O'Hara was yelling at Wes that he'd done enough damage to the soldier, and the scout might have stopped then if another soldier hadn't entered the fray.

Mickey Rafferty had come to America to escape starvation and make a fortune. He'd achieved the first, but his liking for drinking, gambling and women had curtailed any chance of hanging on to the few dollars he'd earned laying railway tracks, cutting down timber, mining for gold and, latterly, wearing cavalry blue. But he did like a fight, and although he had neither affinity with the views of Trooper Jackson nor cause for enmity with Wes Gray, he couldn't resist leaping from his saddle on to the scout's back. He was a heavy man and Wes collapsed under the weight of his forceful and unexpected intervention.

Most of the gathered crowd were offering encouragement to the fighters, enjoying the spectacle more than rooting for a particular victor, but Tommy O'Hara was demanding an end to the contest. Mickey Rafferty had no interest in taking advantage of his opponent while he was face down in the dust, he was looking forward to a toe-to-toe slugging match, so he clambered to his feet and waited for Wes to do likewise. Sergeant O'Hara tried to get between them but Rafferty held him off with an outstretched arm.

'Come on, Sarge,' he said, 'a bit of entertainment for the boys. There hasn't been a good fight on the post for a long time.'

'And there won't be now. It's to the guardhouse for you if you don't remount immediately.'

The Irishman raised a laugh among the onlookers when he answered, 'They've just let me out of there to go and collect the bodies of the officers.'

Distracted by the exchange between the sergeant and Trooper Rafferty, no one took much notice of Jackson, who was getting to his feet. Seizing his opportunity, he swung a blow, double-fisted, into the kidney region of Wes Gray's back. It was a wicked blow, one to which a less experienced fighter might have succumbed. The scout, however, had been fighting for survival all his life and had learned to set aside pain until the fighting was over. He turned to face his assailant, and was just in time to block another double-handed blow that had been intended to strike him on the back of the neck. He delivered his own punch, a short jab which again struck Jackson under the heart.

As the soldier doubled over in pain, Wes Gray pushed him backwards, tumbling him into the water trough. Instantly, Wes reached in and pressed on the man's shoulders, forcing his head under the water. Jackson began kicking, arms swinging like the sails of a windmill and the water bubbling around his face, an indication of his growing panic.

'Let him up, Wes,' ordered Tommy O'Hara. At the same time, strong arms encircled the scout from behind and pulled him away from the water trough.

'Don't kill him, Mr Gray,' Mickey Rafferty's soft lilt sounded in the scout's ear. 'Little men like Jackson aren't worth hanging for.' The words and the expression on Rafferty's face held a hint of amusement and respect.

'What's going on here?' The new voice was stern and commanding. The group that had formed around the fighters stepped aside for Colonel Finch. He looked at Wes Gray, the soaked trooper, and then the sergeant in turn. It was from the last of the three that he expected an explanation.

Instead, it was Trooper Jackson who spoke. 'Wild as the savages,' he said, an accusation aimed at Wes Gray. 'Sooner Custer rids the country of them the better it will be.'

'Custer,' sneered Wes, 'he's only fit for attacking sleeping villages and killing women, children and old men. God have mercy on him if he ever gets into a real fight with the Sioux.'

Silence hung heavily over the group.

Colonel Finch said, 'If you don't intend to help us find Miss Goodwin I want you off the post immediately.'

Wes Gray left Fort Hamilton behind, aware that his outburst against George Armstrong Custer had been a mistake. What he'd said in anger would neither increase his own popularity nor further the cause of the displaced tribes. For most Americans, Custer was a hero, acclaimed as a daring and victorious Civil War fighter, so belittling his abilities wasn't going to win him any friends, especially in a military stronghold on the eve of conflict. To some, in fact, it would heighten their suspicion of him, would question his loyalty, mark him as a traitor to his own kind.

Wes Gray didn't see himself in that light. He was merely a man with knowledge of the customs, mores and needs of the people on both sides of the argument, and he told the truth as he knew it. Custer's claim to be a great Indian fighter was based on just one incident, the defeat of Black Kettle's Cheyenne on the banks of the Washita. The General had boasted of a great victory that had taken the lives of over a hundred and thirty Cheyenne – but the newspaper reports withheld the fact that fewer than twenty of the dead were fighting men and the remainder were women and children. Still, added to his Civil War record and flamboyant character, it was enough to promote the belief that Custer could crush the nomad bands and make the West safe for settlers.

Advancement by white men across the country had been more rapid than anyone could have foretold, and Wes knew that for the people of the Plains an end to their free-roaming hunting days was fast approaching. It was an understanding that provided him with no pleasure, but one that he'd come to accept. Its inevitability now had the effect of diffusing his anger, allowing him to consider his next move with calm deliberation.

Although the band that had ambushed the soldiers was still roaming these hills, Wes thought it unlikely that they would try to attack Caleb Dodge's wagon train. In his opinion, they were too few to have any chance of success, and it was more reasonable to assume that they would go north to join the other fighting groups. To be on the safe side, however, he needed to report what he knew to Caleb as soon as possible – but that didn't rule out spending the night on his farm along the Mildwater Creek. His wife, Apo Hopa, and his partner, old Curly Clayport, would be expecting him.

As he rode east from the fort, past those familiar landmarks that led him home, he also knew that they took him close to the site of Red Knife's village. The plight of Senator Goodwin's daughter troubled his mind. He'd argued with Colonel Finch that there was nothing he could do for her, and that was the truth of the matter, but it troubled him that his animosity towards her father might have influenced his decision. It still niggled him that she'd wanted to visit the Sioux village knowing the soldiers had gone there to drive the people out of their homes, but the three lieutenants were just as guilty for taking her. But it wasn't in his nature to refuse assistance to anyone who needed it, so he turned north before reaching the creek and headed for the village, even though he had a low expectation of finding the warriors and their captive there.

The breeze was in the wrong direction so it wasn't until he was within half a mile of the village that the stench reached his nostrils. The camp was in a ravine that provided water and shelter for the people and grazing land for their horses. It was the grazing land from which the stench arose, and as he came closer he saw it was littered with the carcases of scores of ponies. The entire herd had been destroyed. Grotesque in death, the animals had lately represented the pride and wealth of the village. Now they were carrion. Wes was stung by the wanton slaughter, and his anger was heightened by the message he read in such a deed: the villagers were being forced to walk to the Red Cloud Agency. Many of the old and infirm would die before they got there. It was cruel treatment of people who had tried to live peacefully – was there any wonder if the young men now sought vengeance.

He sat on the rim of the ravine for several moments, watching for movement or any tell-tale sign that any living creature was down there. When he was certain that the girl and her captors were not in the immediate vicinity he rode down the slope and walked his reluctant horse slowly through the gutted village. Every home had been torched, and here and there within their circles he could see the charred bundles of those men and women who had resisted the soldier's invasion.

In the centre of the village, at the place where the men sat in council, a lance had been thrust into the ground. Midway on its shaft, a small medicine bag had been tied. Inside there would be relics, sacred tokens, their meaning significant to whoever had left them. Wes assumed it was the warriors who had taken Annabelle Goodwin, because four arrows had been fired into the ground around the point of the lance. It was a vow of vengeance. The four would fight unto death to avenge the attack on their homes.

Wes waited a moment longer before continuing his journey home. Would the four target the soldiers who had destroyed their village, or would they go north to fight with Crazy Horse? And what hope of survival was there for Annabelle Goodwin?

THREE

Wes Gray slowed the dappled filly to a walk, then halted and let his eyes settle on the lone figure atop the distant crest. Perhaps a mile separated them, too far for specific identification – indeed he needed to use all his knowledge of the mannerisms of people just to know if the other was a red or white man.

Crossing trails with anyone in this lonely area had always been a rare occurrence. Sometimes he'd run into an army patrol out of Fort Hamilton, or a band of Sioux or Cheyenne hunting for fresh meat in hills that once teemed with game, but never before had he met another lone traveller. In past years he'd had no reason to expect trouble from anyone he met – the soldiers knew him as a wagon-train scout whose experience and exploits made him an invaluable asset when negotiating with the tribes, and to the Sioux he was Wiyaka Wakan, Medicine Feather, a brother of the Arapaho, who spoke for them at

Treaty meetings. But now things were different, and he tested the rifle under his leg to ensure it would come easily into his hands if required.

The other rider, too, had paused momentarily, but now began guiding his horse over the rim, then set it to a dead run when he was on level ground. As he drew closer, Wes allowed his rifle to slide back into its boot. Although there was an unusual awkwardness in the man's riding style, the scout was able to recognize Curly Clayport when he was yet two hundred yards distant.

The cause of Curly's graceless riding was apparent when he pulled rein alongside Wes. His face was distorted with bruises and cuts, his left eye swollen shut, so he had to twist his head to make eye contact with his partner. His left shoulder was hunched high to relieve pain in his arm, which he held close across his body. The multiple dark stains that smeared his blue wool shirt were clearly the result of lost blood.

'They took Sky,' he blurted out, answering Wes's question before it could be asked. Apo Hopa's first husband, unwilling to use the Lakota language, had called her Sky; the soldiers and traders at Fort Hamilton still used that name.

'Who's taken her?' Wes wanted to know.

'Soldiers. I tried to stop them, but there were too many.'

'When did this happen?'

'Yesterday. I didn't know what to do, Wes. They weren't from Fort Hamilton, so appealing to Colonel

ENEMIES OF MEDICINE FEATHER

Finch for help seemed futile. There was no one else I could turn to.' He dropped his eyes as though ashamed that he'd been unable to protect Apo Hopa. 'I knew you would be here soon.'

Wes Gray's mind was in turmoil. His first desire was to ride off in pursuit of the men who had taken Apo Hopa, but experience cautioned against hasty reaction. 'How many were there?'

'A sergeant and six men. We thought it was just one of the regular patrols.'

'What did they say?'

'That all Sioux were confined to Agency land. They had orders to kill all hostiles, which Sky would be if she didn't go willingly. I thought they might kill her, Wes. I told them the farm was her home, but they wouldn't listen to me. They were rough with her, Wes. The sergeant knew who she was. I told him she was your wife, but he just laughed at that. "Medicine Feather's squaw," he called her. "Perhaps that's deserving of special treatment," he said to the soldiers who had grabbed Sky, and they all laughed. That's when I tried to get her away from them, but they were too strong for me.'

Wes knew she'd been taken to join Red Knife's people. His instinct was to pursue them and take her back, but it was the army he was opposing, not a gang of law-breakers. He needed to be clever now, not ruthless. Killing soldiers would put both of them on the wrong side of the law.

'The doctor at the fort needs to check you over,'

he told Curly, and they set off together, back to the place that Wes had recently departed.

His sudden return aroused interest among the soldiers who witnessed it. Jackson, with whom he'd tangled earlier, had been relieved from driving the wagon sent to recover the bodies. When Wes and Curly rode through the gates he was gossiping in the shade with a couple of troopers from his unit. A scowl touched his face as the scout rode past but he had the good sense not to re-kindle the argument that had left him bruised and sore. It didn't escape his notice, however, that Wes Gray's companion was more battered than he was himself.

While Curly went to find the doctor, Wes strode into the colonel's office. The orderly opened a connecting door and announced that Wes Gray had returned.

Colonel Finch's response was terse. 'Tell him to get off the post. I don't want to see him.'

Wes pushed his way into the inner office. 'You do if you want any chance of finding that missing girl.'

'Changed your mind?' asked the colonel. One glimpse of the scout's glowering face was sufficient to inform the soldier that whatever had occasioned Wes Gray's change of heart, it had not been inspired by benign thoughts for his predicament. Nor did he have to consider long to understand the anger that was simmering behind the eyes that glared at him.

'You knew, didn't you? When I was here earlier you

knew that Apo Hopa had been taken. Why didn't you tell me?'

Colonel Finch couldn't find any words.

'Apo Hopa is my wife, not a hostile. She should have been safe on our farm, protected by soldiers, not abducted by them. Curly, too, has been badly beaten by those who took her. He's with your doctor now.'

'According to the law she's not your wife.' As the words left his mouth, Colonel Finch knew that they were the wrong words to use if his intention was to pacify Wes Gray.

'Then the law needs to change if you want to see Senator Goodwin's daughter again. Those who took her won't talk to me, won't let me get anywhere near because they've taken a vow against all white men – but they won't harm Apo Hopa. She has been revered by her people since birth, raised among the *wiyan wakan*, the holy women of the tribe, her guidance sought even while she lived with me. She won't be harmed by those who have the Goodwin girl, and is probably the only person who can persuade them to free her.'

Colonel Finch was already aware of Sky's role in Red Knife's village: it had been spoken of on more than one occasion, but at this moment he wasn't completely sure that Wes Gray's suggestion to use his wife's influence with the rogue warriors wasn't just a ruse to get her away from Captain Faraday's special force. A glimpse at the scout's face didn't provide any assistance, all he could see was anger.

'You need to decide quickly,' Wes told the colonel. 'Miss Goodwin has been a captive for several hours.'

'I have men out looking for her.'

'Then I suggest you send a galloper after them and get them back here. The girl will be killed instantly if they get too close.' The soldier sat silently at his desk trying to decide what action to take. 'You need to act quickly, Colonel,' urged Wes. 'Captain Faraday's people are making Red Knife's people walk, but they are a couple of days ahead of me. I ought to catch up with them tomorrow, but then Apo Hopa and I will have to pick up the warriors' trail before we'll be able to find them. The longer you delay, the less chance we have of finding Miss Goodwin alive.'

'I can't be sure that Captain Faraday will release Apo Hopa.'

'Then you'd better make your orders to him clear,' said Wes. 'Spell it out that without Apo Hopa you won't see the senator's daughter again.'

'She might already be dead.'

'That's true, but do you want to be the one who tells her father that you abandoned her to her fate?'

After a momentary pause, Colonel Finch began to write out an order. 'I'll have to send an officer with you to stress the importance of this command,' he said. Wes nodded an agreement. 'And I've written that Apo Hopa will rejoin them after you've found Miss Goodwin.'

Wes Gray's only response was to say that he would

be ready to leave in ten minutes.

The visible cuts, bruises and abrasions, together with a wrenched arm socket, were the extent of Curly Clayport's injuries. Wes was content to leave him in the care of the army medic until he was ready to return to their farm on the Mildwater Creek. In the meanwhile, the wagon bearing the dead officers had returned to the fort, and a handful of men had gathered around the infirmary doorway as though needing to witness the bodies to be convinced of the killings. One or two cast looks at Wes that could have been interpreted as accusatory, but no one gave voice to their thoughts.

Major Shannon had been chosen by Colonel Finch to escort Wes and endorse the signal for Captain Faraday. He was accompanied by four troopers. Wes's questioning look brought the answer that under the current threat of hostilities the colonel had deemed a small detail essential. Wes had another opinion, however, that their task was in fact to enforce Apo Hopa's re-captivity when the fate of Annabelle Goodwin had been established. His view was strengthened by the inclusion of Trooper Rafferty among the quartet. Earlier, the big man had seemed eager for a fight, but in Wes's experience Irishmen often were. Still, he meant to keep a close eye on him.

Dusk was approaching when they left Fort Hamilton, but they ran the horses hard into nightfall. They were twenty miles beyond the site of Red

Knife's village when they made camp. At most, Wes calculated, Faraday's column was equidistant ahead of them. They would catch them early in the morning. Momentarily he was rueful of the decision he'd taken. Had he pursued the soldiers alone when he first learned of Apo Hopa's abduction he would already have them under his observation. He had little doubt in his ability to find his wife among the captives and spirit her away. Even now, they could be fleeing into the night – but to what destination? That had always been the stumbling block. Their home on the V-shaped tract of land would be the first place the soldiers would search, and the wagon train, too, would come under suspicion of harbouring them. By enlisting the help of Colonel Finch he'd hoped to alleviate the threat of agency confinement that hung over his wife, that he'd obtain her freedom in exchange for his services – but the written command marked them as fugitives if Apo Hopa failed to rejoin the people of Red Knife's village.

Yet even as he settled in his blanket for the night, Wes was reconciled to fleeing with his wife after they'd fulfilled his promise to discover the fate of Senator Goodwin's daughter. They would disappear forever. He didn't yet know where they would go, but it would be some place out of reach of soldiers and government men, some place they would never be found.

Wary of a surprise attack by the hostiles, Major Shannon posted a two-hour guard regime throughout the night. It was, however, a snuffle from his own horse that alerted Wes Gray to possible encroachment. His eyes opened wide, instantly awake, but for a moment not another muscle moved. He listened, but could pick up no other sound than that made by the light breeze that disturbed the surrounding trees. Even so, that inexplicable prickle at the nape of the neck that had so often warned him of danger in the past, was again his companion. The lack of further agitation among the tethered mounts removed the possibility that the interloper was a scavenging wild beast. They would all be anxious if they'd picked up the scent of bear or wolf. But men of all the Plains tribes understood horses and knew sounds, gestures and touches capable of pacifying the most nervous animal.

Slowly, Wes moved his head so that he could see across the last embers of the fire. The guard was sitting on the edge of a fallen log, awake though perhaps more mindful of the remembrance of a sweetheart's embrace than vigilant for an enemy's attack. Four bundles, the motionless forms of the other soldiers, lay in a line to his left. Whatever had disturbed his horse, it hadn't come from those with whom he travelled.

Lifting his head higher, Wes sniffed the air. If he'd hoped to catch an alien scent he was disappointed. Only the smell of earth and leaves competing with the odours of the sweat and dung of the horses filled his nostrils. Still, he was uneasy. The dappled filly was looking across at him as though they were the possessors of a secret that must remain unspoken. It seemed clear to Wes that whatever had disturbed the animal had come from the trees behind the picket line. If the Sioux had come calling they wouldn't be satisfied with stealing horses.

Wes had pitched his blanket close to some bushes, and now rolled silently among them. Instantly, he withdrew from its scabbard the bone-handled knife that he kept behind his left hip. Its blade was long and curved in the fashion of the knives made famous by Jim Bowie. He gripped it in his right hand as he snaked around the bush and concentrated his gaze on the thicket behind the horses. For a full minute there was no movement either among the trees ahead or from those behind. No shout sounded from the guard to announce that his reverie had been disturbed by the scout leaving the camp.

Staying low, squirming on his belly, Wes moved stealthily forwards, pausing every yard to check for signs that his advance had been detected. He was in among the trees when the first movement caught his eyes: a figure, human, flitting shadow-like away from him. With evidence of a raid, Wes emitted a yell. Disclosing his own position in such fashion put him at risk, but it raised a warning for the sleeping soldiers whom he expected would come running. Quickly, Wes got to his feet and plotted a route of pursuit. Crouching, running on his toes he covered the ground, all the while casting around so that he wasn't taken unawares by another raider. If these were the band of Sioux who had captured Annabelle Goodwin, then they were at least four in number.

Movement again caught his eye, but in the darkness it was impossible to identify the source. Although he hadn't heard anything, Wes was aware that there was a horse nearby. Its warmth affected the air, telling him it had run hard or journeyed far. His quarry was trying to reach it, and Wes forsook caution in an effort to catch him before he escaped. It was a mistake. As he left the cover of the trees he saw the man had stopped as though waiting for him. He was holding the bridles of two horses.

The second man came at a run from Wes's right, barging into the scout so that they both fell heavily to the ground. Wes lost his grip on the knife, but he was able to get a hand on the other's sleeve thereby preventing his adversary delivering a knife thrust of his own. They rolled and struggled, used knees and elbows as they battled to gain an advantage. Wes twisted the man's arm, forced him on to his face and dispossessed him of the knife but found himself at the mercy of the first man who had now forsaken the horses to intervene on his friend's behalf. From behind, he had trapped Wes's neck in the crook of his arm and was tightening his hold.

Although the man at his back had the most advantageous hold, he wasn't as strong as Wes Gray. Even though he was struggling against that man's effort to throttle him, Wes had maintained his hold on the other man's arm. Now he released it and rammed his freed elbow backwards into the man behind. The man grunted, and as he doubled over in pain Wes jerked his head backwards so that it crashed into the other's face.

A sharp yell and a barely heard crunch suggested to Wes that he'd broken the other man's nose, but he showed him no mercy. Reaching over his shoulder he filled both hands with the others clothing and flung him over his head on to the grass-covered ground beyond. The man beneath Wes, now that his arm was not being twisted up his back, tried to throw the scout aside in a bid for freedom. Unfortunately for him, Wes was quicker in thought and action. The scout had already gained his feet and now turned the man over and threw a punch that left the other senseless.

Through the trees, one man bearing a burning brand, came Major Shannon and two of the troopers.

'What's going on here?' demanded the officer, and by the light cast by the naked flame he gazed at the two men who were almost comatose on the ground.

Both men wore jackets of cavalry blue, and their peaked forage caps, which had come adrift during the scuffle, were on the ground nearby. Their leggings were made of buckskin, and on their feet they wore beaded moccasins.

'Shoshone,' said Wes in a tone of voice that made obvious his contempt for them.

'These men are two of Captain Faraday's scouts,' said Major Shannon.

Scouts usually covered the territory ahead, not where they'd already been, but Wes kept his own counsel. 'How far ahead is Captain Faraday?' he asked.

'Ten miles,' said the one who was shaking off the effects of the punch he'd taken.

'Then get back to him and tell him we'll catch up to him early in the morning.'

FOUR

The group at the head of the line consisted of officers, pennant bearers, bugler and scouts. They rode about fifty yards ahead of the main body of the column, which moved at a pace dictated by the loads the people carried and the needs of the old and infirm. For the purpose of transporting some of those unable to make the journey unaided, men and women had harnessed themselves to the travois contraptions that would usually be attached to their ponies to drag their homes across the Plains. The knowledge that they couldn't sustain such an effort for more than a few days showed clearly in the distorted expressions on their faces, and the decision that must then be made was obvious to the invalid, too.

Alongside and behind them rode the remainder of the troop, hemming them in, pressing home the message that they were no longer free people. Those soldiers who rode the flanks did so with unsheathed carbines, a stark warning that they would shoot anyone who tried to escape. But it would be suicide to attempt to do so. There was no hiding place on the wide-open grassland, and no possibility of out-running a soldier on horseback. Though some yet nurtured a spirit of defiance it was rapidly succumbing to acceptance of the fact that they were a vanquished people. The jeers of the soldiers stung the few young men amid the throng, but there was nothing they could do except endure them.

At first, the fast-riding group coming down the hillside held no interest for the humbled Sioux – more *mila hanska*, long knives, as though more were needed to goad defenceless people to their destination. Their attitude changed when one of the group was recognized. The man in the buckskin jacket who wore a long eagle feather in his hat, reined his dappled filly to a halt and jumped out of the saddle to mingle with the people while the soldiers rode on towards the head of the column.

Several times, the name Wiyaka Wakan was repeated as he searched the faces for that of his wife. Already, many showed the strain of weariness and others were marked by violent blows. He recalled Sergeant O'Hara telling him that most of the fighting men had left the village, and the evidence of his eyes confirmed that. Most of the people he saw were women and children, but scattered among them were the wrinkled faces of the old people. Here and there the face of a young man could be seen, left behind to hunt and protect the village, but now humiliated by capture instead of achieving a warrior's death.

The people had stopped moving, Red Knife coming to a standstill when he became aware that Wiyaka Wakan was among them. It was a decision that found no favour among his military guards. Orders to keep moving were yelled, but the head of the village waited placidly, arms folded across his chest, until the scout had seen him and began to make his way forward.

A mounted sergeant rode forward, placed his booted foot on Red Knife's back and pushed him on to the ground. 'Get up and move on,' he commanded as the chief sprawled on the ground.

'Hey!' yelled Wes. His eyes burning with ice-cold fury, a determination to intervene hastening his stride.

A small hand, instantly familiar to the scout, reached out from among those people he was hurrying past and rested on his chest. '*Ni-kte-pi*,' warned Apo Hopa. When she spoke again her voice remained soft and low so the soldiers wouldn't hear. 'You shouldn't have come for me.'

'You knew I would.'

'Yes.' The pleasure it gave her was denied demonstration. In the current situation there was no place for personal pride. 'But so did they,' she added in a tone barely above a whisper. '*Ni-kte-pi*,' she repeated. They mean to kill you.

His wife's warning fell on deaf ears because Wes was studying her face. A lump, long and black and clearly the result of a blow from some kind of cudgel, swelled above her left eye and her right cheek was split by a livid gash. The latter was so deep that it would leave a permanent scar.

'Who did that to you?' Wes wanted to know.

Apo Hopa ignored his concern, her own worry outweighing the damage that had been done to her body. 'Flee,' she told him. 'I've been brought here to lure you into their trap. Flee, husband.'

'Hey, you!' shouted the mounted sergeant, addressing his words to Wes Gray. 'Get away from those people unless you want to walk with them in chains.'

Curly Clayport had described the sergeant who'd snatched Apo Hopa as a brute of a fellow who'd enjoyed instilling fear. Curly had said 'He laughed at Sky's protests and struggles and my attempt to resist his men, and there was nothing in his features that offered any hope of pity for those in his power.'

Wes eyed the sergeant a handful of yards distant. A glint in that mounted man's eyes betokened cruelty and a belief that he was the indisputable master of the situation.

'Is he the one?' Wes asked.

Apo Hopa didn't speak, her prime concern being to give the soldiers no cause to involve her husband in the difficulties of her people, even though she knew that it was already too late to achieve such a goal. Nonetheless, her silence was answer enough for Wes and he stepped forwards. Apo Hopa tried to restrain him, tried to cling to his buckskin shirt, but to no avail.

The sergeant had transferred his gaze to Red Knife, who was still attempting to rise from the ground. It was only then that Wes realized that the chief's efforts were hampered because his hands and feet were fettered. Red Knife had almost regained his feet when the sergeant put his foot on his back and kicked him to the ground again.

'Why did you do that?' Wes asked, holding in check the anger that stormed within.

'Because it took him too long the first time.' With a leering laugh, he added, 'He needs practice.'

Wes hurried forward and bent to one knee as though intending to help the chief to his feet.

'Leave him,' snarled the sergeant.

But Wes Gray's apparent move to assist Red Knife had been a ruse, a diversionary tactic to disguise his real intent. As he lowered his body between the stricken Sioux leader and the horse he grabbed the sergeant's foot and heaved upwards. With a yell of surprise, the sergeant lost his seat and fell heavily on the far side of his mount. Instantly, giving the cavalryman no time to recover, Wes dived behind the horse and landed on top of him. Instinctively his right hand had formed into a fist, which he smashed against the sergeant's hard jaw. The soldier grunted, his mouth sagged and his eyes momentarily lost focus.

ENEMIES OF MEDICINE FEATHER

Grabbing a handful of soil and grass, Wes pushed it into the other's mouth and up his nose, then held his hand over his face so that he couldn't spit it out. The sound of his voice was terrible to the sergeant when he spoke. 'I am Medicine Feather,' he said, 'brother of the Arapaho and friend of the Sioux.'

Anything else he had to say was interrupted by the swinging butt of an army carbine. Wes's head had been the target of the soldier who held it, but at the last moment a warning shout saved him and he'd rolled away from the sergeant unharmed. The soldier, however, didn't cease his attack. He followed the scout's rolling form, rifle raised with the clear intention of dashing it against his victim's head.

Wes stopped rolling, lay on his back and allowed the soldier to approach. When he was within striking distance he entrapped the other's lower legs between his own and jerked him off balance. The soldier fell backwards, his carbine falling from his hands. Wes Gray reacted with the greater alacrity. Springing to his feet, he retrieved the weapon and without hesitation rammed it into the pit of the trooper's stomach. There was a gargled 'oomph' as the air was driven out of the stricken soldier and he rolled in agony on the ground.

Wes had no opportunity to pause for breath. The sergeant in the meantime had cleared his mouth and nostrils, and was struggling to pull his pistol from the holster on his belt. Throwing himself forwards, Wes crashed once more against the big man, his full weight bearing him backwards until they toppled as one to the ground, the scout atop the soldier. Wes's shoulder struck the other's chin causing his head to collide awkwardly with the ground. A lesser man might have been stunned by the impact, but the sergeant was as tough as he looked. He tried to wrap his arms around Wes, wrestle him from his upper position but was unable. Strong though he was, Wes was no stranger to such fights and was easily able to hold his position.

'I'll kill you,' the sergeant spluttered, but if he was looking for assistance from another soldier to help him fulfil that threat, it was a forlorn hope. The Sioux had gathered around and were standing firm, successfully blocking the efforts of two other troopers who had dismounted in order to reach the combatants. Still, the sergeant was a strong man, and having worked his right leg free from restraint, used it to knee the scout in the back. The resultant pain caused a loosening of Wes's grip and the sergeant took full advantage. Thrusting his head forwards with all the power he could muster, the soldier smashed it into his opponent's breast.

Winded, Wes released his hold and rolled aside. Despite his bulk, the sergeant was quick to react. He was on his feet and aiming a heavy-booted kick at his opponent in an instant. The fight would have been won if it had connected with the scout's head, but despite his suffering, Wes was yet alert for the other's attack. He caught the foot, twisted and pushed, which sent the soldier sprawling on the ground.

Both men regained their feet and closed on each other. The sergeant came forwards with arms wide, making plain his intention of using his powerful body to grip Wes in a crushing bear hug. But Wes was the more agile man and his right arm moved swiftly to deliver a staggering punch under the other's heart. A follow-up blow, a looping left hand, was blocked by the sergeant before it found its target and the soldier turned defence into attack with a vicious swing of his own.

That blow, too, failed to connect, passing harmlessly over the head of the ducking scout. Instantly, Wes landed another solid punch under the other man's heart, and it seemed he would sink to his knees. When he didn't, a thunderous blow to his chin proved successful and he hurtled backwards. Stunned, unable to maintain his balance, he crashed against those spectators who were immediately behind, scattering them aside as he fell to the ground.

Wes Gray didn't give him the chance to continue the fight. He pounced on him, with his knife in hand, the point of which touched the sergeant's throat.

'I should kill you for what you've done to my wife,' he hissed, 'and if you ever harm her or any of her people again I will cut out your heart and feed it to the wild beasts of the hills.'

At that moment strong arms clamped around him

from behind, pinning his arms tightly against his body, preventing his ability to use the knife. A soft Irish voice spoke in his ear: 'Come away, Mr Gray, come away. Are you determined to be hanged for killing a soldier?' Trooper Rafferty dragged him away from the supine sergeant.

Wes shrugged him off – his anger wasn't abated, but nor was his reason consumed by it. When he looked up he saw that the circle that had formed around the fighters was disintegrating as shouts and the sounds of approaching horsemen filled the air. Only Apo Hopa remained motionless, the expression on her face reflecting the same fear that had been uttered in his ear by the Irish trooper.

'What's the meaning of this, Sergeant?' The officer asking the question was a horse-length ahead of four other men of rank, one of whom was Major Shannon. The speaker was a trim man with small eyes and a slim dark moustache above his upper lip. His left hand rested on the hilt of his sabre as though presenting a pose for a sculptor. Although his first words had been addressed to the sergeant, his eyes had been fixed on Wes Gray, and remained on him when he spoke again. 'We've met before,' he said. 'If you've come for the squaw you've had a wasted journey. Like the rest of these people who failed to report to an agency by the end of February, she's a hostile. She's going to the Red Cloud Agency.'

'You've leapt from Lieutenant to Captain in two years. I'd like to think you'd earned the promotion, but knowing that you suppressed information regarding the attack on the Far West so that it was blamed on the Sioux makes me reluctant to think you deserve it. Perhaps you know the right people.' The inference that his rise through the ranks was a reward instigated by Senator Goodwin reddened the man's features but was not refuted.

Wes Gray spoke again. 'But I am not here to listen to a justification for your behaviour, nor to discuss the rights and wrongs of your mission, Captain Faraday, but let me be clear about two things. First, none of these people are hostiles, and those chains you've put on Red Knife should be removed instantly. Second, when I leave here, Apo Hopa goes with me.'

'There's no chance of that, or do you think you can fight every man in this column? Not even a man with your penny-book reputation can hope to achieve that.'

'I don't have to.' He called Major Shannon forwards.

The officer from Fort Hamilton rode up alongside Captain Faraday and handed him the message from Colonel Finch. 'You are urged to comply with these orders with all haste.'

Bristling, Captain Faraday said, 'I don't take my orders from Colonel Finch. I'm under a higher authority.'

'Well, I think you might find that that higher authority will insist that you do what Colonel Finch asks.' Wes continued talking while Captain Faraday read the note. 'You weren't diligent enough back there, Captain. You left behind some young men whose families you have killed or imprisoned and whose homes you have destroyed. You've turned them into avenging warriors. They've killed some of Colonel Finch's officers and they've kidnapped a young woman from the fort. The young woman, I suspect, is the daughter of the person you regard as your higher authority.'

Captain Faraday wasn't the only officer who reacted with a start to the last sentence: the other was a straight-backed, fresh-faced youth.

'You must be Lieutenant Goodwin,' Wes said to him. 'Yes, it's your sister who has fallen into the hands of the Sioux. Could be she's already dead,' he added, pitilessly, 'but if not, I need Apo Hopa's help to save her. The longer the delay the less chance there will be of success.'

It was clear that Captain Faraday was reluctant to comply with the message from Fort Hamilton, not because he lacked sympathy for Annabelle Goodwin's plight – indeed, having met her he'd envisaged a means of hitching his future to Senator Goodwin's wagon – but because he didn't want Wes Gray to triumph over him. In his opinion, the man called Medicine Feather was a fraud, one of those men whose reputation was based on fables that impressed only the crude and illiterate. He regarded him as a hindrance to the nation's advancement, someone prepared to blacken the character of Senator Goodwin rather than acknowledge the bloodthirsty ways of the Western savages. Upon accepting the special duties on which he was now engaged, he'd promised the senator that he would do all in his power to put an end to the scout's interference. He was certain that there would be further rewards if he succeeded. For the moment, however, he couldn't see an alternative to acceding to Colonel Finch's demand.

Wes, meanwhile, was determined to press home his advantage. Captain Faraday's brutal attack on Red Knife's village, his treatment of the Ogallalah people he was herding to the Red Cloud Agency, and the violence occasioned against Apo Hopa were all reasons for his anger and disgust.

'Which of you will inform the Senator that you weren't prepared to do anything to save his daughter?' he asked. 'Will you tell him it was your negligence because you were more interested in destroying a peaceful village than checking for other warriors in the area?'

'Colonel Finch writes that the squaw is to rejoin the tribe at the close of your mission.'

'I'm not responsible for what Colonel Finch writes.' Wes intended his words to further rile the captain, and he was successful. His tone inferred that regardless of the instruction he was determined to keep Apo Hopa away from the Red Cloud Agency.

Ungracious in defeat, Captain Faraday turned his

horse and rode back to the head of the column, followed by his officers.

Along with her father, Grey Moccasin, and Chief Red Knife, Apo Hopa had listened to the exchange between Wes and the commanding officer. When the soldiers had ridden out of earshot he related his discovery of the officers' bodies, and the crude totem that had been constructed with lance, arrows and medicine bag in the razed village. Red Knife supplied the names of those responsible – Young Owl, Wolf Necklace, Long Otter and Ghost – four youths who had gone hunting a few hours before the attack on the village.

'They have not followed our trail,' and added, 'they are not seeking to strike against those who guard us, which means they will join the rest of the fighting men from the village.'

'Gone to join Crazy Horse?' Wes didn't need an answer to that question, instead he posed another. 'What will they do with the girl they've taken?'

'Though we've all been young,' Red Knife replied, 'it is still impossible to know what the young will do.'

Grey Moccasin was more emphatic. 'If they go to join Tashunka Witco only her scalp will go with them.'

Apo Hopa wanted to know why the life of one girl mattered to Wes: 'Do you want her for your woman?'

'No. There is a man in Washington who is my enemy. He is a powerful man who can do me great harm, even though we might never meet again. You

ENEMIES OF MEDICINE FEATHER

are here because he ordered it. I can't fight him, I can't kill him as I would any man who hurt you, so I have to defeat him in other ways. The captive woman is his daughter. He will be in my debt if I return her to him. Perhaps then he will leave us in peace on the Mildwater Creek.'

Despite the turbulence of the previous days, Apo Hopa had reached a decision that she knew would bring sadness to her husband: in this time of trouble, the people of her village needed her – she would stay with them at the Red Cloud Agency. Drawing them aside, she explained her decision to her father and Chief Red Knife.

Red Knife reminded her of the soldier's plan to kill Medicine Feather, that she had been brought among them to lure him into their trap.

'You must go with him now,' both Red Knife and Grey Moccasin urged.

'Get him far away from the soldiers,' insisted Red Knife. 'Wiyaka Wakan has been a good friend. He needs our help and it must be given. Come to the Red Cloud Agency when the woman has been returned to the Long Knives.'

Although reluctant to leave the people of her village behind, Apo Hopa was in agreement that Wes wouldn't be safe while he remained among the soldiers. So she went with him, but kept from him the decision she had taken. Wes, meanwhile, was determined that she wouldn't again be under the control of Captain Faraday or his sergeant.

ENEMIES OF MEDICINE FEATHER

*

As the Fort Hamilton party quit the column, Captain Faraday thought back to his final meeting with Jeremiah Goodwin. It was the senator who had furnished him with the information that Wes Gray had a Sioux wife, and who had suggested using her to lure the scout into a trap. Wes Gray was a thorn in the senator's side and he wanted revenge. Not only had he ruined the riverboat scheme, effectively delaying Goodwin's plans to reap great profit from the Black Hills' gold, but he'd later written a letter to the *Chicago Times* vindicating the Sioux from any involvement in the attack on the Far West, and which, if it had been published, would have had serious implications on his career. Only the senator's association with the editor had kept it out of print – but on another occasion, with another newspaper, he might not be so lucky. Faraday, too, had been named in Wes Gray's letter, and that was the lever that the senator had used to manipulate the young officer.

'If the man called Medicine Feather were to disappear forever,' Goodwin had said, 'I'm sure a great military future will lie ahead for you.'

Recent events, and meeting Annabelle Goodwin, had stretched Faraday's ambition beyond a military future – but freeing himself from the threat of exposure by Wes Gray was still the first step to take. He called forward Sergeant Watts who was still sore at being bested by the frontiersman.

'At the moment I can't touch that man or his squaw,' said Captain Faraday, 'but if and when they rescue Miss Goodwin they must pay for their insults to the army. Can you handle it?'

'Alone?'

Captain Faraday thought of the two Shoshone scouts who had bungled the job the previous night. They'd expected to find Wes Gray in lone pursuit, but when they'd found their quarry with an army patrol had been retreating, although not quickly enough, to seek fresh instructions.

'Take the scouts Toshawa and Half Face with you. They are good trackers. You'll need them.'

FIVE

They stopped beside a narrow but deep rivulet to rest and water the horses. There had been little conversation between Wes Gray and Apo Hopa since leaving her escorted tribe, primarily because of the urgency with which they travelled, but also because the presence of Major Shannon and his troopers deprived them of all privacy. So close, in fact, had the soldiers been to the heels of Wes and Sky's mounts that despite the scout's warning that Annabelle Goodwin would surely be killed if soldiers were sighted by those who held her, it was apparent that Major Shannon had orders not to let them out of his sight. Somewhere along the trail they would need to part company, but when Wes spoke about it the major argued otherwise.

'My orders are to make sure that Miss Goodwin is returned to Fort Hamilton and Sky to Captain Faraday.'

Exasperated, Wes explained the situation again.

'It's unlikely that Miss Goodwin is still alive. If she is, it will be because her captors are camped somewhere close to their old village and are using her as their slave. But when they choose to move on, which they'll do at the first sight of a blue uniform, they won't burden themselves by taking her with them.'

'I have my orders,' said Major Shannon.

'Then you're going to have to decide what is most important to you, sticking to an order that will ensure the failure of your mission, or hanging on to the small chance of getting the captive safely back to the fort by trusting Apo Hopa and me.'

Later, as he crouched on the bank swilling the dust from his face with the stream's cold water, the matter still had precedence in Wes Gray's thoughts. One of the soldiers approached and knelt beside him: it was Mickey Rafferty, who dipped his neckerchief in the stream, then used it to wipe his face.

'There must be some Irish blood in you, Mr Gray,' he said. 'Only a fool or a son of Galway tries to fight an army single-handed.'

'You don't think I'm a fool?'

Rafferty grinned. 'I know you're not a fool, Mr Gray.'

Wes studied the man. Back at the fort they'd almost come to blows but now the man seemed almost friendly. 'What's your game, Rafferty? At Fort Hamilton you were ready to fight with me.'

The Irishman laughed, the sound a low rumble. 'I'm ready to fight you now,' he said. 'Man, I like a good fight, and I reckon you'd turn out to be the best opponent I've ever had, but there's no malice in it.' He shook his head. 'You don't remember me, do you, Mr Gray?'

Wes Gray shook his head.

'Three years ago I was in California hunting for gold up near the Oregon border.' He paused, allowing Wes time to reflect on that information. 'The Beeston Mine,' he added.

Wes recalled the occasion. He'd rescued four prospectors trapped inside their workings by robbers who'd used dynamite to block the entrance while they ransacked the hut for dust and nuggets. Wes had interrupted them, killed two before the rest fled. Bare-handed, he'd create an air passage through the rock fall before riding to the nearest town for assistance. 'You were one of the miners?'

'I was. You quit the place before anyone was able to reward you for what you did.'

Wes waved aside the thanks.

'No, Mr Gray. We'd have died that day if you hadn't taken a hand. You surely enjoy a fight.'

'I take it the mine didn't yield a big payday.'

'Sure it did,' grinned the Irishman, 'but I left my fortune back at my Philadelphia mansion while I beat my backside black and blue on a Union saddle.'

Uncharacteristically, Wes was unable to respond to the soldier's quip with a smile. Too many serious thoughts engaged his mind: the safety of Annabelle Goodwin, and when that was resolved, Apo Hopa's future, not to mention the plight of the Sioux people and the lingering threat from his distant enemy, Jeremiah Goodwin. He rubbed the excess water off his face with his hands, and would have walked away, but Rafferty retained his attention with a few more words.

'Blind obedience to orders is the mark of a good soldier,' Rafferty said, 'and Major Shannon is a good soldier. Me, well I'm not so good. I only enlisted for two years, and that's up in a few weeks. We've been told to keep a close eye on you, which isn't difficult in this country.' He cast a look all around the open prairie land, making the point that even if Wes and Sky made a break for it they would still be visible for miles around. 'The army always thinks it knows best, Mr Gray, even if they've needed to bow to your knowledge in the past. If you say that the sight of a uniform will put the young woman in greater danger, then I believe you, but even if you're doing this just to get your own woman away from Captain Faraday's men, I reckon I still owe you my support. Be ready, I'm sure you'll get a chance to give us the slip.'

The urgency to pick up the trail of the four young warriors was tempered by the need to escape the vigilance of the soldiers. Apo Hopa confirmed Wes's suspicions that if the braves who had killed the soldiers had not yet fled north to join Crazy Horse, they would have taken refuge among the low hills close to the site of their razed village. They were young men, not much more than boys, and likely to choose a familiar place while they planned their next move. A water source and good grazing would be their priority, and in the hills there were many such places to choose from.

There was perhaps an hour of daylight left when, after fording a shallow stream at the foot of those hills, Wes brought the group to a halt. From this point on he knew there was a chance of being observed by those they were seeking.

'From here we must go on alone,' he told Major Shannon, and another argument loomed when the officer made it clear he wasn't going to give the scout any leeway. It was Mickey Rafferty who prevented it developing. He had dismounted and lifted one of his horse's forelegs, checking its shoe and feeling a fetlock.

'Beginning to limp, sir,' he told Major Shannon. 'He hasn't picked up a stone so it must be a strain. He'll be all right if we don't ask any more of him today.'

The major, at first irked by the trooper's intrusion, quickly grasped that it presented him with an opportunity to withdraw from a possible clash with the scout. He allowed himself to be swayed by Rafferty's concern for his horse, and issued an order to make camp in a voice of stern authority that was meant to establish his command of the entire party.

Rafferty, whose head had been bowed over his mount's leg and who was murmuring soft words like a mother tending a sick child, looked up and met Wes Gray's eyes. He winked, then set about unsaddling the horse.

When darkness fell, the soldiers ate their rations while clustered around a small fire. Wes and Apo Hopa sat apart from them, he explaining that in order to avoid recapture she might have to travel west with the wagons. Meanwhile, she worked with a collection of twigs she had gathered from the ground. She was twisting them together, creating a circular framework which wasn't much more than twelve inches in diameter.

'Ghost and Wolf Necklace know me,' she told Wes, 'but the other two are younger and I've had little contact with them. I will cover this *wahacaka*, this shield with the colours of the four portions of the world, a symbol that can be used only by the spiritual leaders of the village. Even if they don't recognize me they will know I am a holy woman and allow me to approach unharmed.' She added that at daybreak she would gather red and yellow flowers, the representations of east and south and in the meantime she borrowed the feather from Wes's hat for the white north, and twined strands of her own black hair among the plaited twigs to represent the west.

Escaping the watchfulness of the soldiers was still uppermost in Wes Gray's thoughts, but once again, as the group settled into their blankets for the night, Major Shannon imposed a rotational two-hour sentry duty on his troopers.

'The success of their first attack might persuade those hostiles to try again,' he told Wes.

The scout wasn't deceived – he knew that the main purpose of the guard was to make sure that he and Apo Hopa didn't flee while everyone slept. He waited until the soldiers had rolled out their blankets beside the fire before selecting the place where he and Apo Hopa would sleep. Aware that he was constantly under the surveillance of a wary Major Shannon, he selected a site that put twenty-five yards between them. It was slightly uphill and in a natural delve in the ground that was thick with long grass. When pressed down it provided a soft bed. He knew the officer was agitated by the distance of separation, but he also knew that there was nothing the other could do about it. He and Apo Hopa were not prisoners, nor were they under military command.

Apart from the comfort provided by that delve, Wes had selected the spot for another reason: it put them closer to the horses, and if an opportunity arose to escape the soldiers' vigilance, then they would be better placed to take advantage of it. Major Shannon, however, was an experienced officer, and counteracted Wes's move by changing the sentry's post to a point that was more advantageous for keeping an eye over the sleeping camp than it was for detecting the approach of an outside force. Wes noted the change and gave consideration to their chances of crawling away during the darkest part of the night and reaching the horses undiscovered. If it could be achieved, then their chances of defecting from their military escort were favourable. He spoke the Lakota tongue when he told Apo Hopa to get some sleep, but to be prepared to move instantly if there was a chance to flee.

Wes Gray, too, slept awhile. He knew that if their first attempt to flee failed they wouldn't get a second chance. So it was essential to await the right circumstances before making a move. For two reasons he dismissed all thoughts of absconding during the first guard's shift. Firstly, it was unlikely that in that period the suspicious Major Shannon would be settled into anything but the shallowest sleep, and secondly, there would still be a glow from the campfire. The best opportunity would be during the second or third spell of guard duty when the blackness of night would be at its deepest. It also meant that if their absence wasn't discovered until daybreak, he and Apo Hopa would have been gone for several hours. In such a case, searching for them would be a hopeless task. So he slept because he needed the rest.

Sounds reached him that disturbed his slumber. Low voices, someone coughing as the next man began his spell of sentry duty. Wes's eyes opened and he was looking directly at the spot assigned as the guard post. The silhouette of one man could be seen with his rifle sloped against his shoulder, while that of another man could be observed making his way towards the place where the other three soldiers were lying. One of them raised a head. When it was turned in his direction, Wes figured it belonged to Major Shannon. After a moment it was lowered again, and following a few moments of shuffling sounds, coughs and wheezes from the relieved guard, silence settled once more over the camp.

Wes wondered how long he needed to wait before waking Apo Hopa. His belief that Major Shannon would be a light sleeper had been verified by the officer's awareness of the change of guard. It emphasized the need to exercise the utmost caution when they did make their move. Perhaps thirty minutes had passed before Wes thought the time was right, but just as he began to reach out a hand to awaken Apo Hopa there was movement from the place where the guard had been stationed. The soldier was on the move.

Initially Wes thought the man was merely stretching, warding off a tendency towards sleep. Without raising his head, Wes was able to watch the man's progress as he made his way silently to the place where his comrades lay sleeping. Perhaps he hoped to find some coffee still warm in the pot among the ashes, but that idea was swiftly removed from the scout's mind as the soldier paused only momentarily. When he continued his journey with the same stealthy tread it took him outside the scope of Wes Gray's vision. Reluctant to raise his head, Wes pressed his ear to the ground in order to detect the man's location. Lying in the delve proved to be a handicap to this effort, especially as the man was moving with intentionally soft steps.

It was the low sound of hoofs scraping the ground that informed Wes that the soldier was behind him and among the horses, though for what purpose, the scout had no answer. There had been no previous disturbance among the animals to draw the sentry's attention to them, so once again, there seemed little option for Wes but to believe that the sentry had enforced the patrol on himself to stay awake. Still, he slipped his knife from its sheath and waited, all senses on full alert. He remained still and waited. Even if the man returned to his original post, Wes knew that he couldn't risk trying to leave the encampment during this man's stint of duty. Beside him, Apo Hopa, who was facing in the opposite direction, stirred gently.

Two minutes passed before Wes sensed a furtive approach to the delve in the ground where he and Apo Hopa rested. He tightened his grip on the bone-handled knife while calculating the distance by which they were now separated. The man was on the lip of the indentation, now in a position to strike if that was his intention. Instead, a low Irish voice whispered through the darkness and grass.

'Mr Gray,' said Mickey Rafferty.

Wes turned to face the soldier, his eyes wide open.

The soldier grinned. 'Figured you'd be awake,' he said, and with a nod towards the knife that was held in meaningful fashion, added, 'and ready for flight. Everyone's asleep. Now's your chance to go.'

With the lightest touch, Wes found Apo Hopa's shoulder. Her eyes, too, were wide open, as awake and ready for flight as her husband. Earlier, Wes had given her a knife, which could now be seen gripped firmly in her right hand. When Rafferty saw it, it pressed home to him the knowledge that if an offensive approach to the pair had been his intention, it would have proved futile.

'I come in friendship,' he whispered to the young Lakota woman, then, speaking to both, told them to leave their blankets on the ground. 'I'll make it look as though you are asleep. Perhaps no one will know you've gone until daybreak.'

No time was wasted. Wes didn't even saddle his horse, but carried the equipment on his back while leading the animal clear of the small encampment. They headed west into the hills, secure in the belief that no one among those left behind was capable of following their trail among the valleys and along the ridges they intended to travel.

SIX

The defection of Wes Gray and Apo Hopa wasn't discovered until sunup, when the soldiers were stirred awake at the end of the last man's guard duty. Some were eager for breakfast, others, as was their habit, had grumbles to voice concerning the discomfort of a night outdoors – but when a fire was lit and coffee brewed, all were equally ready to face the day ahead.

True to his word, Mickey Rafferty had arranged the blankets of the absconders to give the impression that they were still asleep in their grassy delve, and the ruse worked well enough until one of the troopers was sent to summon them to breakfast. Due to Mickey Rafferty's assertion that all the horses had been present when he'd made a circuit of the camp during his stint as sentry, the irate Major Shannon was led to believe that Wes and Apo Hopa had been gone no more than three hours, instead of the actual five. Even so, troopers Smith and Tuttle were on the receiving end of his angry tirade, because the wagon-train scout and his Sioux wife were capable of

ENEMIES OF MEDICINE FEATHER

covering many miles in three hours.

As expected, when he questioned them, there wasn't a man in the detail who possessed any tracking ability. Major Shannon, however, had been issued with orders: if alive, Annabelle Goodwin was to be taken back to Fort Hamilton, and in any eventuality, Apo Hopa was to be returned to the custody of Captain Faraday. Shannon was an officer in the US Cavalry, so fulfilling those orders was his first priority – and if he was to avoid returning to the fort empty handed, his only course of action was to find Wes Gray and his wife. Within minutes of the discovery of their flight, the soldiers were in the saddle and making tracks away from their campsite.

'Where are we going, Major?' Mickey Rafferty wanted to know.

'To the Sioux village. That's where Wes Gray intended picking up the hostiles' trail. Perhaps there'll be enough signs for us to follow.'

Mickey Rafferty didn't reply. He knew it was unlikely that they'd catch up with the man called Medicine Feather, which suited him well enough. Besides, if they rode around in circles out here it was possible that by the time they got back to Fort Hamilton everyone would have forgotten that he was meant to be in the guardhouse.

Sergeant Watts and the Shoshone scouts had been surprised the previous day when Major Shannon's party had made camp with daylight still available for travelling. Rather than make their presence known, they'd retreated a mile and found a coulee deep enough to keep them hidden from those ahead.

In the morning, Toshawa made his way forward on foot to observe the morning preparations of Major Shannon and his men. When he returned to Sergeant Watts it was with surprising news.

'Wiyaka Wakan is no longer with the soldiers,' he reported. 'He and his squaw have gone.'

Sergeant Watts wanted to know which direction the soldiers had taken.

'Perhaps towards Fort Hamilton,' he was told.

'Well, you come with me and we'll find out their intentions. Half Face,' he said to the other Shoshone, 'have a look around their camp. See if you can find any sign of another trail, then come and report to me.'

It took only the time needed for Sergeant Watts to saddle his horse before he and Toshawa were racing across the meadowland, closing quickly on Major Shannon's detail.

'Captain Faraday sent me to escort the squaw back to our column when the senator's daughter has been found,' Sergeant Watts told Major Shannon. 'Where is she now?'

'She and her husband slipped away in the night. We hope to pick up their trail at the Indian village.'

'Perhaps my scouts can be of assistance,' said Sergeant Watts. 'They are good trackers.'

Half Face rode up at that moment and, catching

the sergeant's eye, gave a slight nod to let him know he'd found evidence of the route taken by Wes and Apo Hopa.

'You're going in the wrong direction, Major. Let Half Face and Toshawa find them. They'll break a twig and turn a stone here and there so that we can follow them. Wes Gray and his squaw won't get away. She's Sioux, and he lives like he's one of them, and the Shoshone hate the Sioux more than we do.'

Although Wes had told Major Shannon that picking up the trail of Annabelle Goodwin's captors entailed returning all the way to Red Knife's destroyed village, Apo Hopa was able to avoid that necessity, thereby saving them a great deal of time. Instead, she led the way to Deer Creek, a place that would be on the young braves' route, whatever their future intention. Either they would cross the narrow stream to go north to join the warring bands under Crazy Horse, or, if they meant to stay close at hand to harry the soldiers of Fort Hamilton, they would follow the watercourse into the high ground where there were many secret lairs in which to feed and rest.

When they reached Deer Creek, Apo Hopa's assumption proved correct. Either confident that there were no soldiers in the vicinity to trouble them, or because they were fleeing with reckless haste, the four young braves had done nothing to obscure the marks on the ground that announced they'd been here. Although the marks were two days old they were clear to read. No one else had passed this way in the meantime, and the hoof prints of ponies and two shod animals showed clearly in the softer earth at the water's edge. In addition, a couple of moccasin prints could be seen alongside those of the animals – but there was nothing to indicate that Annabelle Goodwin had been allowed to drink at the clear running stream.

Wes knew that it was merely conjecture to assume that as a prisoner she'd been restrained, perhaps tied to a horse while the braves refreshed themselves, but it was a reasonable thought, and one that provided a straw of hope if he wanted to believe that Annabelle Goodwin was still alive. He tried to banish from his mind the thought that her body had been discarded somewhere along the back trail from the village. But he knew that there was nothing to be gained by guessing the girl's fate – he would learn the truth when they caught up with her captors.

Because there were no other visible signs on that side of the water, Apo Hopa rode slowly across the stream and examined the ground on the other bank. 'They did not cross,' she told Wes. 'They have gone into the hills.' She looked upstream then started her mount in that direction.

Realizing the Sioux youths had finally added caution to their flight by riding single file in the stream, Wes and Apo Hopa rode parallel along opposite banks looking out for where they had left the water. They had covered almost two miles of steadily rising terrain before they discovered it. They'd reached a meadow of lush summer grass, coloured with an array of wild flowers. Ahead of them, hills arose in high smooth mounds.

'There are many valleys among those hills,' said Apo Hopa. 'One of them is known to few people outside our village. It is a place in which we hid horses from our enemies. I think they have gone there.'

'Let's go, then,' said Wes.

'Wait,' he was told, and Apo Hopa dismounted.

She spent a few minutes collecting a handful of flowers that had opened wide with the warmth of the sun. Wes didn't recognize the red flowers, couldn't put a name to them, and the yellow ones he'd only ever heard referred to as 'monkey flowers', but after Apo Hopa twisted them into the twigs of her rudimentary *wahacaka*, its decoration and symbolism was complete. She held the little shield in her hand when they rode on.

For more than an hour they travelled, here and there espying tell-tale signs of those of whom they were in pursuit. The day was hot and energy-sapping, but they continued vigorously in the knowledge that they were getting closer. Relief from the sun came when they dropped below the brow of a hill that offered a descent into a valley. They were a third of the way down when Apo Hopa reined in her mount to a sudden halt. Wes stopped beside her, didn't speak, waited for an explanation. Her demeanour demanded increased vigilance on his part. He had known other occasions when her senses had borne a forewarning. Now, head held high, she seemed to be struggling to catch a scent, a sound, a sight that would confirm a dreadful suspicion that hung tantalizingly outside her grasp. Her eyes were wide and her voice heavy with incredulity when she spoke.

'Susuni.'

'Shoshone!' Such a declaration took Wes by surprise, and when he glanced at his wife he could see that she, too, doubted the word she'd uttered. There had been no indication that the hills were inhabited by anyone other than those they were seeking, and as though providing proof of that belief, at that moment his eyes alighted on a movement on the hillside below. He pointed. 'Look,' he said. 'Not Shoshone. Lakota.'

The youth was astride a white-faced sorrel pony and was carrying a lance and shield in his left hand. Almost at the same moment that he'd been seen by Wes he'd become aware of the scout's presence on the hillside. So quickly did he turn his horse and race away through the flimsy tree cover that he didn't know the other was not alone.

'That is Long Otter,' observed Apo Hopa.

'Let's go,' said Wes, eager to learn the fate of Annabelle Goodwin.

'They are young, and to them you are a *wasicun*. They will fear you. Let me do the talking.'

Unhurriedly, Apo Hopa led the way down the

slope, her unbraided hair partially restrained against the tug of the warm breeze by a rabbit-skin head band. She wore a long, beaded doe-skin shirt over fringed leggings, and in her hand she carried the multi-coloured shield. When they were close to the valley floor she raised it high, clarifying the sanctity of her status among the people.

Three near-naked figures stood in a group before a low, crude shelter that had been constructed with branches and blankets to provide shade from the day-time sun as well as night-time shelter. They wore breech-clouts and moccasins, but no other clothing. A dozen long animal teeth were fastened around the neck of the foremost of the trio. He was the tallest and eldest, perhaps three years older than the other two, who stood a couple of steps behind. Dried blood smeared his face and body, boasting of his victory, and two fresh scalps dangled from the lance that was gripped with both hands in war-like fashion. It was also decorated with a length of maroon ribbon that had once formed a bow in a young woman's hair. Sternly, he awaited the approaching riders.

Behind him, the others held bows but showed no desire to use them. Wes guessed they were no older than fourteen, and still considered themselves more in danger of a scolding from a holy woman than they were from physical combat with her companion. He was surprised by the absence of rifles – he knew that they possessed them because there had been bullet holes in the bodies he'd seen. Perhaps they'd recognized Apo Hopa and didn't consider firearms necessary, or perhaps they'd been caught unawares, their youth and inexperience awarding them insufficient time to gather the guns from the shelter – or perhaps the missing fourth brave was nearby and squinting at him along a barrel.

Without turning to look at her husband, Apo Hopa identified the group fifty yards ahead. 'Wolf Necklace is the leader,' she said softly. 'Long Otter and Young Owl stand behind.' They advanced only a few more paces before stopping. 'Wait here,' she said as she slid from the back of her mount.

Apo Hopa spoke to the young braves about their relatives who were being shepherded towards the Red Cloud Agency, told them how proud they had been when Wiyaka Wakan reported their victory over the soldiers, but now urged them to reunite with the village.

'There are dark days ahead,' Sky told them, 'and the grandfathers and infants need the protection of every brave and strong warrior.'

Wolf Necklace tried not to be swayed by the flattery. Their plan, he insisted, was to find Apo Hopa's brother and the other warriors from their village who had gone to fight with Crazy Horse.

In the meanwhile, Wes was trying to learn what he could about the situation. A circle of ashes showed where a cooking fire had blazed. Rabbit bones and scraps of pelt were scattered nearby. An inexperienced hand had butchered and skinned their food, and carelessly cast aside the waste. Despite their recent victory, it was clear that Wolf Necklace was leader of an unfledged band. But Wes hadn't forgotten the purpose for seeking them out, and there was little to suggest that Annabelle Goodwin was still alive. The maroon ribbon wrapped around Wolf Necklace's lance had surely belonged to the senator's daughter, although he knew that neither of the scalps that accompanied it belonged to her. Major Shannon had told him that she had long, fair hair, the opposite to those that fluttered in the light breeze. Perhaps she was still alive, but Wes knew that her scalp could just as easily be a prized possession of one of the other young warriors.

Trees were plentiful along the low slopes and provided ample cover and ambush points. Wes swept them with only a cursory glance. Apo Hopa's presence was surely a guarantee of his safety. His main point of focus was the mix of ponies and cavalry horses forty yards to his right. Although untethered, they were clustered together, as static as a grazing herd, though none of them had their head down to eat grass. One or two gave the occasional start, which led to snorts and head shaking. Wes was quick to discern the cause of their odd behaviour: someone was hiding among them, and he had no doubt that it was the fourth Lakota youth. Ghost, Wes assumed, was the best marksman, and hiding among the animals kept him close enough for an accurate shot if it became necessary.

Ahead of him, the discussion between Apo Hopa and Wolf Necklace was proving fruitless. The young warrior was only willing to speak about the raid on their homes and the bodies they had found of Little Owl's family, Young Otter's mother and his own brother.

'We will kill all *wasicun*,' he insisted.

Wes Gray stepped down from his horse, unstrapped his gunbelt and hung it over the saddle.

'Do you think you can kill me, Wolf Necklace?' he asked. 'I am American, but I have killed many enemies of your people.'

'I know you, Wiyaka Wakan, and I am not afraid of you.'

Apo Hopa flashed a look at Wes that demanded patience. Wolf Necklace was proud because he'd killed his first men in battle. Although the others in his band were not much more than boys, he was now their leader and wanted to demonstrate his bravery to them. It would wound him to be disgraced in front of them.

'We didn't come here to fight you or punish you for killing the soldiers. We seek the girl you captured.'

Wolf Necklace remained silent, facing Wes with cold determination.

'Where is she, Wolf Necklace, what have you done with her?'

Still Wolf Necklace remained silent, but he changed his grip on the lance to hold it in a more threatening manner. Young Otter, too, began to raise his bow.

Wes snapped a warning at the trio. 'I haven't come to fight you, but I will if you try to use those weapons. And I'll kill you.'

At his side, Apo Hopa spoke to them softly. 'It is Red Knife's command that the white woman should return to her people.' She gestured slightly with the decorated shield to emphasize her authority to speak on behalf of their chief.

Wes watched them closely, saw the tension ease from the muscles of their shoulders and the expressions on their faces. He knew they were afraid of him, but he also knew that it was reverence for his wife that would prompt their decision. Still, he needed to establish his domination among them. He pointed towards the horses and spoke gruffly to Wolf Necklace. 'I know someone is hiding among the horses. Tell him to join us. If you don't, I'll assume he means to shoot me, but I'll kill you before he does.'

Wolf Necklace stared at Wes, but still remained silent.

Wes turned away and headed towards the horses. 'Ghost,' he called, and when there was no immediate response, he shouted again.

Although not as tall as Wolf Necklace, Ghost was of similar age, and his body, though lean, suggested that he had inherited that tough, wiry strength that was typical of the men of his nation. He pushed at the rump of one of the ponies to clear himself a way through, but didn't look at Wes: like the younger boys, he'd accepted Wolf Necklace as his leader, and it was to him that he looked, seeking approval for emerging from his hiding place.

Ghost wasn't carrying a rifle. Instead he held a plaited grass rope, which Wes guessed was attached to one of the ponies, because he yanked it as he came forwards. But Wes was wrong: with hands bound at the wrist and the other end of Ghost's rope around her neck like a halter, Annabelle Goodwin stumbled forwards.

Her clothing was torn and scruffy, and her face, partially veiled by long, swirling fair hair, was dirty and bruised. The tautened skin of her cheeks spoke of exhaustion and exposure to demands and conditions of which she had had no previous knowledge nor expectation. She had been used as all female slaves were used, had been forced to labour almost beyond endurance. There were dark marks of blood on her dress, but Wes guessed that most of it had come from the rabbits she'd been compelled to skin and butcher before cooking them. She fell to her knees, and when Ghost pulled at the rope again she sprawled face down on the dusty ground. The sob she emitted spoke more of fear than pain.

Wes Gray quickened his stride. His knowledge of the Lakota language was sufficient to enable him to speak to Ghost in his own language. 'Untie her,' he called, his voice harsh and commanding.

Behind him he heard Apo Hopa speak his name. Her voice wasn't loud, but the caution it contained didn't escape him. It was a reminder that, although the boys were young, he had no authority over them. In addition, even if their deeds didn't match his own, they were still due the respect of fighting men. They had taken the scalps of their enemies, which was a mark of manhood throughout the Lakota nation, and Wolf Necklace had been chosen as their leader, so the treatment of their captive was in his hands.

Ignoring Apo Hopa's warning, Wes threw another demand at Ghost for Annabelle Goodwin's release. Again, that youth looked beyond Wes, seeking instruction from his leader. It was immediately obvious to him that Wolf Necklace didn't want him to release their captive, because Wolf Necklace was now running towards Wes Gray, the lance gripped with both hands with the clear intention of running it through his body.

For Annabelle Goodwin, the arrival of a white man had instigated a spark of a belief that her ordeal was about to end. Because he'd only spoken in the Lakota tongue, she hadn't understood his shouted words, but his gestures had needed no explanation. He was her salvation, her hope of rescue, so when his own safety came under threat, desperation forced from her a shout of warning.

The captive girl's shout of alarm hadn't been necessary. His senses attuned to the situation, Wes was alerted to the young brave's attack by the disturbance of the air around him and the faint sound of moccasin-clad feet across the ground. He turned in time to avoid the thrust aimed at his stomach. Ranging his hands alongside those of Wolf Necklace, he grasped the lance and they matched their strength. It was an uneven affair, Wes Gray having an advantage in weight and experience. Disarming his opponent wouldn't have been a difficult matter even though the young buck was resisting with grim determination.

Apo Hopa said, 'Husband,' in such a way that conveyed her fear that Wes would kill Wolf Necklace. He heard her plea to spare the youth, but wasn't sure it could be done without shaming him. He twisted the lance, almost broke the other's grip, then relaxed to allow Wolf Necklace to recommence the struggle.

'Wolf Necklace is strong and brave,' he declared, so that his praise could be heard by those standing nearby.

As though invigorated by his opponent's words, Wolf Necklace braced his legs and used all the strength in his upper body in an effort to force Wes Gray backwards. He stared into the white man's eyes. 'She is my woman,' he said.

Wes wasn't surprised by the intensity with which Wolf Necklace announced ownership of Annabelle Goodwin. Clearly, she hadn't been kept alive for her skill in the preparation of food, nor for her strength as a substitute pack animal. If the former, the camp site wouldn't be littered with animal waste, and if the latter they wouldn't still be in these hills. No, brutal though it had undoubtedly been, taking scalps had not been Wolf Necklace's sole claim to manhood, and Annabelle Goodwin owed her survival to her soft skin and fair hair.

While maintaining the pseudo struggle, when Wes spoke again he lowered his voice so that only Wolf Necklace could hear him. 'I must take her back to the fort,' he said.

'No,' said Wolf Necklace. He tried to trip Wes by hooking his left leg around the other's right, but failed.

In response, Wes, willingly fulfilling the move that Wolf Necklace had attempted, went down on his back, and using the lance they were both holding and placing his right knee in his opponent's stomach, hurled him over his head. Casting aside the lance, he jumped to his feet and ran at the rising Sioux youth. His impetus carried them both fifteen yards so that they were well away from the others. No one attempted to interfere – all were anxious about the outcome.

Wolf Necklace tried to work his knife free from its sheath, but Wes used the edge of his hand to chop at the youth's wrist, causing him pain. Then he pushed him to the ground, using sufficient force to roll him even further from the watchers.

'I don't want to kill you, Wolf Necklace,' he muttered, 'but when I leave here the white girl will go with me.'

ENEMIES OF MEDICINE FEATHER

Anger twisted the Sioux's face. 'She is mine.'

'She's no good for you,' Wes replied. 'She can't prepare food, and she is too weak to carry even a medicine bag. You must leave this place soon or the long knives will find you, and you know the white girl will be a hindrance if you try to take her with you. To escape the soldiers you will have to kill her, and then they will be more determined to catch you. Let her go with me now, and lead your band out of these hills as quickly as you can.'

'She is mine,' he repeated, but with less determination.

Lacking any desire to harm the young brave, Wes resorted to cunning, and when he spoke again it was with flattery as though he'd been duped into a situation from which he would exit the loser. 'So, Wolf Necklace is not only strong but is also wise. He wants to bargain for his trophy and will demand a high price.'

Somewhat confused, Wolf Necklace remained silent.

'I have this knife,' Wes said, 'but your captive is young and worth more than that.' He rubbed his chin as though in deep thought. 'My grey,' he said, 'is a better horse than any in your string. She is yours in exchange for the girl.'

It showed in Wolf Necklace's eyes that negotiating a bargain would prevent a loss of face, but the white girl was a trophy he was reluctant to part with.

'A young buck with two scalps will be much

admired by the young women of his village,' Wes said, planting a thought that could convince Wolf Necklace to accept the deal.

Perhaps that thought was already lodged in Wolf Necklace's mind, perhaps his brief contemplation was centred on one special maiden among the people of Red Knife's village, so when Wes allowed him to get to his feet, the deal was agreed. When they rejoined the others he assured everyone that Wolf Necklace was not only a brave and strong fighter, but a tough trader, too. The dapple, he told them, was the best horse he'd ever had.

Apo Hopa advised the four to rejoin the people of their village who were heading towards the Red Cloud Agency. 'You'll be able to slip past the night guards,' she told them, 'and your families will be pleased to know you are safe.' If the younger boys appeared to listen keenly to what she said, they seemed to be even more swayed by the argument she next put forward against their fight with the army. 'In death,' she said, 'the long knives multiply. For every one that is killed another ten follow. Their army will grow until they kill every warrior. Then what will become of our nation if every man is killed? The women will grow old and wither, and the Lakota people will be no more. Return to your homes,' she pleaded, 'learn, and become leaders of the new ways by which we must live.'

'We will join Crazy Horse,' insisted Wolf Necklace. The younger boys had listened keenly to Apo Hopa advocating a return to their parents – she was a holy woman and therefore deserving of their attention – but they didn't demur. Wolf Necklace was their chosen leader. Whatever disappointment Apo Hopa experienced remained hidden. They were Ogallalah, war was in their blood.

Wes was allowed one of the cavalry horses that had been captured during their raid on the picnickers, but he had to share it with Annabelle Goodwin. The Lakota youths knew that they would need spare horses to complete the long ride ahead.

SEVEN

At the top of the hill, Wes looked back into the valley. His last piece of advice to the boys had been to ride north with all possible haste, but he could see them gathered around the grey dapple, inspecting it for defects like seasoned horse-traders, or Indians who'd been fooled by white men in the past. At another time, their antics might have given him cause to smile, but loitering put them in danger, and he had found himself unable to be amused since the discovery of gold in the Black Hills. And the loss of a good horse didn't help, especially when the cause of it hadn't ceased complaining since they'd parted company with her former captors.

Annabelle sat sideways on the saddle, while he balanced on the rump of the cavalry horse as they climbed to the brow of the hill. She'd refused to ride with Apo Hopa, who, in common with the practice of her nation, had only a blanket between herself and her mount – but the look she'd cast at his wife told

Wes that she nursed other objections. Indeed, when he'd climbed up alongside her, it was clear that she had objections to his nearness also, but he had no intention of walking.

'You're free now,' he had told her when he climbed up alongside, 'so stop mewling like a whipped dog and hold your head high. Show them defiance and pride.'

But her head remained sunk on her chest and her cheeks were wet with tears as they left the boys behind.

'Be quiet,' he told her, but it had little effect, and from time to time, at each inevitable contact of their bodies, he could feel her flinch.

'You should have killed him,' she muttered. 'You should have killed all of them.'

When they dropped down the far side of the hill they reached the stream that would lead them back to Deer Creek. There was no need for haste, so they dismounted among some trees, ostensibly for the benefit of the horses but in reality to give Annabelle Goodwin some moments of privacy in which to compose herself. Wes left the women and took the animals downstream to drink. He heard Annabelle's raised voice before he'd had a chance even to loosen the cinch on the cavalry horse, and hurried back to investigate.

Annabelle was shouting at Apo Hopa: 'Stay away from me. I don't want any of your kind near me!'

Apo Hopa heard the footsteps behind her and

turned to intercept her husband, but Wes brushed aside the attempted restraint of her arms. He gripped Annabelle's left arm and pulled her forwards.

'You've had a rough time,' he said, 'but forget about yourself and think about the bodies at the destroyed village you were so eager to see. That was the work of your brother and his soldiers. And look at the cuts and bruises on Apo Hopa's face. They were made by those same soldiers. Yet she came here to save you, and you wouldn't have survived if she hadn't. Do you understand what I'm saying? You owe your life to Apo Hopa.'

An angry Wes Gray was a daunting sight for most men, and for Annabelle Goodwin he seemed no less terrible than the four ferocious Sioux who had covered their hands and faces in the gore of her picnic companions. No one had ever before berated her with such blunt criticism, and his assertion that she should be grateful to such a person as an Indian squaw was repellent to her. But he wasn't done, and while he spoke she quivered before his blazing gaze.

'Times are hard, Miss Goodwin, but you've survived. On the frontier, everyone suffers. You need to put your pains behind you and learn to blame those who made you suffer, not those here to help you. Pride and defiance, Miss Goodwin. The Sioux prize these qualities, and you need to adopt them.'

The gruffly delivered exhortation was too much for the senator's daughter. With tears running down her cheeks she turned away to hide herself among the stream-side trees. Apo Hopa, who had listened to Wes's outburst with surprise, spoke to him.

'I do not recognize my husband,' she said. 'I do not know this warrior who has so much anger in his heart. It is not the custom of Wiyaka Wakan to growl like a wounded grizzly at one in need of his help.'

'She has thoughts only for herself,' Wes replied. 'She doesn't see your injuries, nor would she care about them if she did.'

'That is true, but the marks left on me by the blows of the soldiers will soon disappear. The white woman is not only in pain, but is also shamed by her treatment at the hands of Wolf Necklace.'

'I know what Wolf Necklace has done to her, and perhaps the other braves, too, but she's free of them now and has a rich home in the east to return to. What about you, Apo Hopa, and our future together? The army's intention is clear: they mean to persist with their plan to imprison you in order to punish me. After delivering the girl to the fort we will have to make a dash for freedom. I can't leave you in our cabin on the Mildwater Creek, that's the first place they'll search. So we'll have to go far away, perhaps live in the mountains until they lose interest in us. We'll be fugitives, Apo Hopa, but I won't let you fall into the hands of soldiers again.'

Apo Hopa saw the fire in Wes Gray's eyes, knew that he was willing to fight to the death to keep her safe. Such passion only made more difficult the task of telling him that she couldn't go with him. Indeed, her own pain at parting would be equal to his, but she knew she could no longer withhold from him her decision to join her people at the Red Cloud Agency.

Wes was stunned to silence when she told him that their place along the Mildwater Creek could no longer be her home. 'I want to return to my people.'

A Sioux woman had the right to leave her home at any time, whether the fault was with her husband or because there was someone else she'd rather be with. Wes had always known that to be the case, and knew, too, that the husband must accept the situation without complaint. Even so, if Apo Hopa hadn't continued talking he would have found it difficult to remain silent.

'It was known at my birth that the Spirits of our people favoured me. I was raised in the ways of the *wiyan wakan*, the holy women, and only allowed to marry you because it was believed that forging a bond between my people and yours would be good for our village. But we have failed, Wiyaka Wakan. It is clear that our people will always be divided. Now there is no joy for my people, and if I am not with them, there cannot be joy for me. It is time for me to be the person the Spirits meant me to be.'

Anger, for which he had no explanation other than the knowledge that he was embroiled in events over which he had no control, had been growing within Wes for several weeks. Senator Goodwin's desire for revenge was, perhaps, part of the problem, but he was sure that the source of his unease was something greater. Now, Apo Hopa's declaration of their failure probed at the heart of it. For several years he'd tried to foster understanding between the red man and white, had aided both sides and earned their respect. He'd been acknowledged as having a foot in both camps, someone who could be trusted to negotiate and mediate with fairness. But that trust, it seemed, had dissipated, and on all sides, he figured, he was viewed with suspicion. No one was certain which side he would choose if it came to a fight, and war, they all knew, was looming large. Apo Hopa, it appeared, knew the choice that she must make no matter what her husband decided to do. Although he'd always known that the needs of her people would have precedence over her own happiness, Wes had never truly believed that she would ever be faced with such a choice. Now, as he studied her face of stony resolution, he realized she'd known that this day had been fast approaching, and despite the personal cost, had long been prepared for it.

'My people need me, so I will return to them after the white woman has been returned to the fort,' said Apo Hopa.

Although he was forced to accept her decision, Wes was still concerned for her safety.

'I'll accompany you to the Red Cloud Agency,' he told her. 'I don't trust Faraday to protect you, and like Senator Goodwin, he's an enemy I am unable to fight.'

'You said that rescuing the girl would put an end to their enmity.'

'Perhaps it will,' said Wes, but he wasn't sure he'd ever believed that to be true. It was a hope that had been engendered by the need to rescue Apo Hopa from captivity, a wish to restore her to an untroubled existence in their home in the Mildwater valley – but the army's determination to get her to the Red Cloud Agency was a clear indication that that would never have been permitted. They would have been forced to find another home, someplace further west where they could escape the notice of the military and Wes's political enemies. But Apo Hopa's decision to return to her people had put an end to that course of action, although it didn't quieten his fears for her safety. Jeremiah Goodwin, he suspected, might still choose to punish him through her.

He no longer believed that Jeremiah Goodwin's animosity towards him would be alleviated by the rescue of his daughter – the senator, he believed, wasn't the kind of man to acknowledge a debt to another. Annabelle Goodwin had been abused by her Sioux captors, but her father, Wes believed, was more likely to accuse him of being the perpetrator of offences against her than hail him as her saviour. Wes judged him to be the sort of man who would have preferred the death of his daughter to an obligation to protect her from any stigma arising from such an experience. Whatever words he used in public, Jeremiah Goodwin would want a scapegoat, someone

ENEMIES OF MEDICINE FEATHER

to suffer for any actual or perceived society or business snub, and Wes Gray fitted the bill.

Stressing his fears for her safety, Wes insisted that he wouldn't allow Apo Hopa to rejoin her tribe until they had reached the Red Cloud Agency.

'I'll travel with you,' he told her. 'I don't want you on the open range in the clutches of Faraday's soldiers.'

It was at that moment that the sounds of gunfire reached them from the far side of the hill they'd recently crossed. The shots were sporadic, fighting was prolonged.

'Stay here,' Wes ordered and sprang on to the back of Apo Hopa's saddleless pony, which was more suited to the hill country than the big cavalry horse.

Annabelle Goodwin, unkempt and face streaked with dried tears, approached from her isolated streamside spot. Her gaze was fixed on the hill, the expression on her face inquisitive as to the meaning of the shots that could be heard. Wes figured she imagined it was a troop of soldiers searching for her. Perhaps she was right.

'Remain hidden among these trees no matter who comes out of those hills,' Wes instructed. 'I'll be back soon.' He kicked his heels against the pony's flanks and was soon picking out a route to the summit.

Minutes had passed since the last gunshot had reached his ears, and Wes suspected that the fighting had come to an end. Only two possibilities occurred to him as to the cause of the conflict, one as unlikely as the other. Either the four Ogallalah braves were battling among themselves, or Major Shannon's detail was more adept at following signs than he had considered possible. Nothing that had taken place while he'd negotiated Annabelle Goodwin's freedom had indicated the likelihood of the former – and besides, in the event of a dispute, Sioux warriors went their own way, they didn't kill each other. And although Apo Hopa and he had travelled as quickly as possible, they had taken elementary precautions to hide their route since leaving Deer Creek. So before reaching the crown of the hill where he would be visible to those on the other side, he dismounted and crawled the last few yards on hands and knees.

At first, the only movement that caught his eye was provided by the horse group that now included the bartered dapple filly. Like their owners, the patience of Sioux ponies knew no bounds. They would wait and watch as though senseless of events around them until action was required, then they would be alert, fast and brave. At the moment only the occasional toss of a head or swish of a tail indicated that they were not asleep on their feet. Wes, however, was conscious of the fact that all were faced in one direction. As though in anticipation of someone emerging to attend to them, the focus of their attention was the crude assembly of branches and blankets that had been built by the young warriors. Guided by this, Wes shifted his gaze towards that place – but before he could focus on it he saw the first body, that of one of the younger boys, Young Owl, he believed. It was face down, twisted in one of those awkward shapes that are only sustainable in death. Wes figured Young Owl had been trying to reach the shelter where, perhaps, the rifles were kept.

Wes continued to scrutinize the scene below, and his keen eyesight quickly picked out a second victim draped in a forked tree. The torso hung forwards, the arms almost touching the ground. Its slenderness convinced Wes that he was looking at the body of Ghost. For several seconds he continued to scan the killing ground, but could see neither signs of life nor more bodies. The lack of movement on the hillside tended to dismiss discovery by the army. Soldiers were rarely able to remain still and hidden for long, the more especially following a successful assault that had halved their enemy's force.

On the other hand, he told himself, if the dispute had involved only the four young Sioux, then where were the victors? Perhaps they hadn't escaped the conflict unscathed either, perhaps they were inside the shelter tending their wounds. Until he had evidence of the fate of Wolf Necklace and the other younger brave, Wes was reluctant to descend into the valley. Making the shelter the focus of his attention, Wes narrowed his eyes against the brightness of the sun and attempted to penetrate the depths of its darkness.

Then, surprisingly, the detection of a shape within

the shelter coincided with a movement on the hillside below him. A rifle barrel had been pushed out from the low, dark hiding place, the ensuing gunshot breaking the silence. The bullet whined as it bounced off a hillside rock, causing the figure in a cavalry blue jacket to drop out of sight. To Wes, the man's reaction had carried the suggestion of a practised manoeuvre, as though the soldier had deliberately presented himself as a target in order to draw the enemy's fire, but that seemed unlikely. The army didn't normally use such rash tactics and Major Shannon didn't strike Wes as the kind of officer who would stray from the military book of tactics. But Wes was beginning to wonder if he had misjudged Major Shannon – he was already amazed that he'd been able to get his men to this location so quickly.

As the reverberations of the gunshot died away, Wes became aware of a second soldier on the floor of the valley. He'd made his way downhill far along the valley so that the crude structure stood between him and the horses. The trees from which he emerged put him at a point slightly behind the opening of the Sioux shelter so that he was out of the eye-line of anyone inside. Pausing momentarily to cast a glance uphill, he began to cover the separating distance. He moved stealthily, loping in a style that was unusual for any white man. Before he'd taken five steps Wes was able to identify the man, and knew that his earlier judgement hadn't been in error. Major Shannon's detail hadn't traced him to this place. The man he was watching was one of Captain Faraday's Shoshone scouts.

When they'd first reached this valley Apo Hopa had sensed Shoshone in the vicinity, but the sight of Little Owl had chased her suspicion from their thoughts. This wasn't Shoshone territory, and there had been no reason to believe that they were under threat from a raiding party, but Wes knew that the warning should not have been ignored. Apo Hopa's instincts were faultless. He blamed himself for allowing his reactions to become dimmed by the anger that had overtaken his spirit. Even now, knowing that the men in soldier uniforms were Shoshone scouts, that quickness of thought and decision that had saved him in many situations now eluded him.

The man on the valley floor raised his rifle above his head and Wes knew it to be a signal to the other scout that he was ready to attack. Instantly, the scout on the hillside showed himself and again dropped out of sight when Wolf Necklace's rifle spat lead.

Wes Gray was Medicine Feather, brother of the Arapaho and friend of the Sioux. Many times he'd proclaimed that their fights were his fights, their enemies his enemies, and he had lived by those words. Crow and Shoshone were the greatest foes of the Lakota people, and his instinct was to intervene on behalf of Wolf Necklace. But he didn't. He thought of Apo Hopa's recent remark, that her people and his would never be united; he recalled the attitude of some of the soldiers at Fort Hamilton, the suspicion of him that showed on their faces. Perhaps the time had come to admit that he couldn't represent both sides, that the time for diplomacy had gone: he must choose the side for which he would fight.

But even in the minor skirmish that he was currently witnessing, it wasn't an easy decision to make. Instinctively he wanted to help the Sioux youths, but irrespective of his personal feelings, he had to acknowledge that the cavalry scouts were doing their duty. Wolf Necklace and the others had slain soldiers, and meant to kill more. They were hostiles. If Wes interfered and killed the army scouts, then he, too, would be hunted by the army, and no matter what service he'd given in the past, he would still be hanged as a traitor.

The scout on the hill fired two shots at the shelter, forcing whoever was within to keep their heads down. At the same time, the other Shoshone darted the last few yards to the mouth of the shelter and fired into it, ejecting shells and pulling the trigger time after time. Casting aside his rifle, he reached inside and dragged the body of Wolf Necklace into the daylight. With a war shout of victory, he drew a knife from beneath his jacket and scalped the dead Sioux youth and used it to signal to his companion that the battle was over. While the other hurried downhill, the slayer of Wolf Necklace moved towards the body of Little Owl, but didn't stop to lift the available trophy. Instead, he skipped over the young brave, dropping to his knees at a point twenty yards beyond, making it difficult for Wes to keep him under observation.

Transferring his attention to the other scout who had now reached the floor of the valley, Wes watched as he scalped both Ghost and Little Owl. Wes knew it was against regulations for an Indian scout to take scalps, but he figured that the desire to prove success over a despised enemy was no less prevalent in a Shoshone warrior than it was in the Sioux. The dead Sioux may have been young and inexperienced in battle, but their scalps had the same value as any other when attached to a shield, lance or coup stick.

When he rose to his feet, Wes could see that the first scout had another scalp in his hand. The fourth body, that of Long Otter, lay obscured from view behind a ridge of long grass.

Together, the scouts kicked apart the shelter, spreading the twigs, branches and blankets over a wide area. They picked over the items that had been within, collecting the ammunition pouches and rifles that had been taken from the dead officers. Then they turned their attention to the horses, which remained silent and watchful away to their right. One of them was pointing at the dappled filly and the other lifted one of its front legs, revealing an iron shoe. The two raised their eyes to the hillside, pointing at the path Wes and Apo Hopa had descended to reach the floor of the valley.

Although he couldn't hear their conversation, Wes

wasn't at a loss to interpret their gestures and signs, because when they had lifted their heads, he'd recognized them and known why they were in this valley. He'd made a mistake: he should have interfered on Wolf Necklace's behalf. He should have killed the scouts when he'd had the opportunity, because he now knew that they were under orders to kill him. They were the scouts under Captain Faraday's command with whom he'd already tangled, and clearly they had been sent to kill him and Apo Hopa once Annabelle Goodwin was free and safe. Now they had recognized the dappled filly, and had probably guessed that it had been used to barter the release of the senator's daughter. Killing four inexperienced Sioux had been a bonus for them: now they would be coming for him.

EIGHT

Certain that the Shoshone scouts had been sent to kill him, Wes Gray cast aside his reluctance to do battle with them. He was prepared to kill anyone who threatened his life or that of Apo Hopa. He had warned the big sergeant who had manhandled his wife that he would cut out his heart to feed to the wild beasts if he ever harmed her again, and he'd meant every word. He might do the same to these two Shoshone who were hunting him. He regretted that he'd ignored his instincts earlier, knowing that if he'd acted then he might have saved the life of Wolf Necklace. That mistake he had to clear from his mind: the focus of his endeavours now had to be his own survival, and Apo Hopa's, too.

Speed had been the priority when he had left Apo Hopa and Annabelle Goodwin at the stream to investigate the gunshots, and in order to be better able to tackle the hill climb, he had used Apo Hopa's blanketed pony instead of the harnessed horse he'd taken in exchange for the dapple. The result was that he now lay on the ridge without his rifle, and the distance to the valley floor meant that his enemies were out of range of his revolver. Besides, they were currently inspecting the horses that had belonged to their vanquished foe, making it impossible to get a clear shot at them. But now that he was aware of their presence in the vicinity he wasn't going to allow them to pursue him any further. Somehow, before they left these hills he had to kill them.

Observing them for a few minutes, Wes became aware that a quarrel was developing between the Shoshone scouts. It didn't take a great deal of intelligence to work out the manner of their dispute. Horses were a sign of wealth among all the tribes of the Plains, and one of the men was reluctant to leave the mix of unshod ponies and shod horses behind. It was clear that Wes's dapple was the attraction – even Shoshone, it seemed, had an eye for a good horse.

Eventually they moved away from the little group of animals and began searching the ground for signs that would tell them the direction taken by Wes, Apo Hopa and Annabelle Goodwin. Because Wes and Apo Hopa had not considered caution to be necessary, their route up the hillside was soon found, and when the scouts' eyes followed the line to the summit they were looking at the place where Wes lay undetected. They exchanged a few words, then one of them found a length of rope that he used to bind together the rifles they'd collected. The other one, meanwhile, had begun to climb the hill, following a diagonal course that took him away from Wes's location.

'Going for their horses,' Wes told himself, and knew that tackling them separately gave him the best opportunity for success. His first instinct was to overpower the scout in the valley and await the other's return, but he wasn't sure he could descend unseen. Armed as they were with rifles, he knew he would have little chance of success if he got trapped between them. But he couldn't wait until the climber had disappeared over the rim of the hill before making his move, because he would be back with the horses before Wes had reached the valley floor.

The better option was to drop back behind the hill and try to beat the climber to the horses. He didn't know where they were, or how much ground he needed to cover to get to them, but he would be able to move more quickly than the other man, who faced a steep ascent. Wes backed away and retreated down the other side until he found his own mount. For a moment he considered using it to cross the hillside, but was aware of the risk incurred by doing so. If the sound of hoof-beats carried to the other side of the hill, they would give the climber warning of his presence. He began running, long careful strides, mindful of the uneven terrain and the loose rocks and stones that shifted under his feet.

More than half a mile he covered, ever watchful for the horses that he knew must be somewhere ahead, and also alert for the arrival of the Shoshone scout whom he supposed must be somewhere close to the top of the hill. He'd adopted the running style of his blood-brothers, the Arapaho who hunted among the wooded stretches of the Green River, an energy-saving lope that ate up the ground quickly and which he could maintain for long stretches. Although he had no reason to suspect he was under observation from any other enemy, he still used the few trees, high boulders and overhangs that marked his route to cover his progress. As he ran, he regarded each one as a marker attained, but although ready to use it for concealment if the need arose, he passed it without any apparent interruption to his stride.

The crown of a cavalry blue hat jutted above the edge of the hillside, giving Wes warning of the arrival of his adversary. Twenty yards separated them as Wes swiftly dropped to the ground behind a grassy knoll. He was sure he hadn't been seen, but his presence didn't go totally unnoticed: the place where he lay was on the lip of a delve in which the scouts' horses were tethered, and one of them snorted, the way horses do when startled. Wes lay still, not knowing if the scout would interpret the sound as a note of alarm, or a welcome for his return. It was a cavalry horse, one from Captain Faraday's remuda, so it was possible that it knew the Shoshone no better than it knew Wes. Seconds passed in silence. Wes tried to pick up the Shoshone's tread, but if he was moving it was with the stealth of a mouse.

A jingle of harness and a low, guttural utterance reached Wes, informing him that the scout was busy with the horses. He didn't know the Shoshone language, but there was nothing in the man's tone that suggested he was suspicious of attack. Merely pacifying the horse, Wes suspected.

Gingerly he peered over the top of the knoll. He recognized the scout, his nose still swollen from their last encounter. He was moving around the head of the nearest horse then knelt at its forelegs, his back to Wes.

Surreptitiously, Wes slid his wide-bladed knife from its scabbard, then rose to his knees. Gathering his feet under him, he prepared to spring on to his enemy. The horse at whose feet the scout Toshawa crouched suddenly threw its head high. As Wes launched himself forwards, the Shoshone turned to face him: put on guard by the horse's behaviour, the army scout was ready for an attack, and while crouching, he'd filled his left hand with dirt and now flung it at Wes's face. If the throw had been accurate, if the grit had filled Wes's eyes and impaired his vision, Wes wouldn't have seen the knife in Toshawa's other hand and would have fallen on the blade. As it was, a combination of Toshawa's inaccuracy due to a left-handed throw and the use of his forearm to deflect most of the dirt away from his face, enabled Wes to avoid the killing strike. Instead of falling on the blade, he managed to twist his body away from his foe and instead crashed against the horse.

As the animal shied away from the contact, Wes fell to the ground, but although he jarred his shoulder on impact he still retained the grip on his own knife. Intending to end the fight swiftly, Toshawa dived forwards, hand raised to drive the knife it held into Wes's body. Wes clasped the other's wrist, halting its downward motion. His face twisted in a fearsome snarl, Toshawa tried to break free, but was forced to divert his energy to his own defence. Wes's arm was swinging in an arc that would have driven his knife into the Shoshone's side, but it was grabbed by Toshawa and the wrist gripped in like manner to that which was a restraint on his own attack. For several moments they were at impasse, neither able to free their trapped hand in order to impale the other.

Toshawa was first to gain an advantage, suddenly finding the freedom to rise to his knees. Being above his opponent seemed to present him an opportunity to press his weapon into Wes's chest, but he lacked the brute strength with which to do it. Instead, Wes twisted his arm, first to the right then the left and finally pushed the scout backwards, sending him tumbling across the ground. Both men sprang to their feet and, with each knife pointed at an opponent, they circled slowly, anti-clockwise.

Wes lunged and Toshawa jumped back. Again they circled, and again Wes lunged and forced his opponent back. There was now a tree only two steps behind Toshawa, and he would collide with it if forced further back. Keeping his eyes fixed on those of the Shoshone scout, Wes spoke.

'I am Medicine Feather,' he said, 'brother of the Arapaho and friend of the Sioux. Their enemies are my enemies.' A feint with his knife fooled Toshawa into anticipating a slash across his torso. He chose to avoid it by leaping back, but when he did his shoulders struck the tree. He seemed to bounce off it, as though pushed by an unseen hand. Stumbling forwards, he fell on to the point of Wes Gray's knife and died with a terrible gurgle in his throat.

Although it had been a desperate fight, Wes had no reason to believe that the scout in the valley below had any knowledge of it. The struggle had taken place on the back side of the hill therefore couldn't have been observed by the other Shoshone, and no matter how keen his hearing, no sound of their conflict could have reached him. Time was Wes's only concern. Toshawa had come to collect the horses, and the other man would become suspicious if he didn't soon return.

He was now in possession of Toshawa's rifle, but he dismissed all thought of taking out his opponent with a long-range shot. It was an unknown weapon to him, and failing to kill him with the first shot could lead to a protracted gun fight that might attract the attention of Major Shannon's detail. Besides, shooting from ambush wasn't his way. He would get close to his enemy. Kill him face to face.

Wes cleaned the blade of his knife on the ground

before re-sheathing it. Then, quickly, he stripped the body of its army tunic and blue cavalry hat. When he replaced his buckskin coat with it, the tunic was tight across his shoulders, but he figured it might act as a disguise long enough for him to get close to the other scout. He fastened his coat and hat behind the saddle of one of the horses, then mounted the other. With the hat pulled forwards and his shoulders hunched to bring his chin to his chest, most of his face was concealed from view. With the lead rein of one horse in his hand he climbed on to the other, and made his way over the edge of the hill.

After bundling the rifles together, Half Face spent a few minutes going from body to body in search of trophies, as was due to any victor. A necklace of animal teeth was the only item worth taking. Apart from a length of maroon ribbon that fluttered on a lance stuck into the ground, he found nothing of interest either when he searched through the scattered remains of the shelter. Although the ribbon would have been a good gift for Toshawa's sister, he didn't take it. He knew it must have belonged to the missing white woman, so being in possession of it could lead to trouble.

Following a successful raid it was customary to burn the possessions that couldn't be carried away, and for a brief moment Half Face felt compelled to do that, but there had only been one miserable shelter here, and no one would be returning to it.

ENEMIES OF MEDICINE FEATHER

A glance at the hillside revealed Toshawa's descent. Half Face turned his attention once more to the Sioux ponies. Usually they were the first object of a raid, a better prize than slaves, and he shared Toshawa's desire to take them and increase his wealth among his own people. But the soldiers wouldn't permit it. They would become part of the troop's horse herd, and he and Toshawa would never see them again. So the decision he faced was whether to slaughter them or let them roam free. Half Face studied the dappled filly whose tracks had led them to this valley. It stood apart from the group, a couple of hands below the height of regular army mounts, but like Indian ponies, being lower made it more suitable for tackling the hilly terrain. He appreciated the deep chest that promised stamina, the firm legs that indicated speed and the graceful form with a high-held head that denoted intelligence. It was watching the horses that were approaching from the hillside.

Half Face's attention was caught by a pile of harness that was stacked against a tree close to the horses. He began to move towards it, but the drumming of hoof beats told him that Toshawa had reached the floor of the valley and was making haste in his direction. He threw a glance in that direction, paused a moment as though puzzled by what he saw, then continued on his way to inspect the saddles that had been worn by the captured cavalry horses. Then he stopped again, wondering why Toshawa was riding the wrong horse. Why was he sitting in Half Face's saddle when his own mount was alongside, apparently sound in wind and limb? Perhaps he would have been alert to a threat to his safety more quickly if his mind hadn't been occupied with the problem of what to do with the horses, but the impression that Toshawa appeared taller when sitting on another horse was slow to develop in his brain.

By now, the rider he believed to be Toshawa had reined to a halt, his head turned aside as he plucked from the ground the lance that had been planted there in order to display its attached trophies. It was difficult for Half Face to make out the features of what he believed was his companion, but he reacted with surprise when he caught a glimpse of a light-coloured shirt beneath the rider's cavalry tunic. Toshawa wore a blue shirt of standard cavalry issue.

Suddenly suspicious, he asked 'Who are you?' – wishing he hadn't left his rifle near the pile awaiting collection. His hand was moving to the holster on his hip, struggling to unfasten its buttoned-down flap, his urgency marring his ability to do it successfully.

Wes lifted his head so that the other could see his face. In his hand he now held Wolf Necklace's lance in menacing fashion.

'I am Medicine Feather,' he said, 'brother of the Arapaho and friend of the Sioux. Their enemies are my enemies.' He kicked his heels against the horse's flanks and charged at the Shoshone scout.

Before Half Face was able to draw the revolver

from its holster the lance had been driven clean through his chest. He died on the ground, the shaft protruding high above him, the maroon ribbon stretching out in the light breeze.

NINE

'Why has he left us?' Annabelle Goodwin wanted to know as she watched Wes Gray race away towards the hillside.

'To know the reason for the guns,' Apo Hopa told her.

Emboldened by Wes's departure, Annabelle Goodwin gave voice to her hope that soldiers had found the camp beyond the hill and were killing 'those savages'. When she added, snappily, 'All of them,' her accompanying glare made it clear to Apo Hopa that she meant the whole Sioux nation. 'Why must we stay here?'

'Because my husband told us we must wait.'

Annabelle Goodwin's scowl expressed her sentiments well enough. The lack of sympathy shown by Wes Gray was only to be expected from someone who'd taken an Indian wife. He was no less a barbarian than those who had been her captors. 'If there are soldiers on the other side of the hill,' she declared, 'I'll go back with them.'

Still holding to the belief that the feud that existed between Wes and Senator Goodwin would be eased when her husband's part in the recovery of his daughter became known, Apo Hopa told her that they would take her back to the fort. 'You must tell your father that you are alive and free because Medicine Feather came for you.'

When the Sioux had made their swift and sudden attack on her picnic party her first stab at retaliation had been to scream that she was the daughter of Senator Jeremiah Goodwin. But in those first few bloody moments she became aware that her father's name and reputation were completely valueless. The sharp blow that had rendered her almost senseless was the first indication that there would be no leniency out of respect for the gentility of her eastern lifestyle, and what followed were three days of terror and abuse that seemed to be a whole lifetime. Being the apple of her father's eye counted for nothing, and although she was sure he would have people searching for her as soon as he was told of her abduction, hope of ever being found had almost disappeared until the arrival of Wes Gray and Apo Hopa.

For three days she'd prayed for rescue from the dirt and ignominy of captivity, promising God in those dark moments of pain and shame when death seemed but a moment away, that if spared she would never again be troublesome to her father nor stray from the safety of the splendid mansion that was her Washington home, where she was surrounded with luxurious furnishings, good food and fine clothes. It was a place of music and laughter, parties and balls attended by people of high society. Her father's associates were all men of rank who wielded political, military or financial power, and who had sons of consequence who were ever eager to pour words of courtship in her ear.

Now that she was free, however, her homecoming took on a different hue. When details of her abduction were revealed her reputation would be forever ruined. She would become a social outcast, a pariah marked with the stigma of disgrace, struck off every invitation list in the city. The line of prospective grooms that had grown with every social assembly would disappear overnight.

But it was the effect that it would have on her father that troubled her most deeply. He loved her, she had no doubt about that, but she was also aware that she was a bargaining chip in his quest for power. She couldn't count the times he'd told her that prettiness such as hers wasn't to be wasted, that the husband she chose from among her suitors must enhance the family's prosperity. Who would marry her now?

Deeply occupied with those thoughts, Annabelle barely heard the gunshots that carried from beyond the hill. Apo Hopa, however, listened to them with the trepidation common to any wife whose husband's life is in danger. But she was also concerned for the four young braves of her village and wondered at the identity of their attackers. Like Wes, she had dismissed the idea of their military escort tracking them. Without her husband to guide them she doubted that they had the ability to find the way back to Fort Hamilton. However, twenty minutes after the last gunshots had reached her, she was forced to re-assess her opinion.

She had been watching for her husband's return, her attention fixed on the hill beyond which he'd ridden, but the sound of horses' hoof beats that now reached her came from the south, along the route from Deer Creek. More than a half-mile separated them from the stretch of woodland in which she and Annabelle Goodwin were hidden, but the blue uniforms marked their identity unerringly. Although their features were indistinguishable, she had no doubt that that it was the group from whom they'd parted during the night. She moved closer to the horse and placed a hand over its muzzle. If it picked up familiar scents it might betray their position.

Apo Hopa's cautious behaviour had caught Annabelle Goodwin's attention, and her interest aroused, she came forward to stand alongside the Sioux woman. 'Soldiers,' she said, the word spoken with a catch in her throat that betrayed emotion. Men in uniform represented the society she understood, were a guarantee that the horrors of the previous days were now at an end. 'They must be looking for me,' she said. 'We must let them know I'm here.'

'No,' said Apo Hopa. 'We must remain here.'

Apo Hopa's insistence was spurred by something more than an adherence to Wes Gray's parting instructions. Although she still believed that returning Annabelle to Fort Hamilton would end the feud between her husband and his enemy in Washington, she had now seen something else, something that made her thankful for her inherent caution. The faces of the soldiers had been indiscernible when the group had first come into view, but that hadn't stopped her identifying Major Shannon by his straight-backed riding style, nor the round-shouldered stoop of one of the troopers, confirmation that it was the detail who'd ridden with them from Captain Faraday's column. But when she counted them, the group had grown from five to six.

The additional soldier was riding alongside Major Shannon. He was a big man, burly, his physique recognizable to Apo Hopa even though his features were not clear. She wouldn't soon forget the punishment that Sergeant Watts had inflicted on her.

'We should join the soldiers,' said Annabelle Goodwin. 'They've come to rescue me. They'll take me back to the fort.'

'No. Let them go. We must wait for Medicine Feather. He will get you safely to the fort.'

Annabelle made a grab for the horse's bridle as though she meant to mount it.

'Don't,' said Apo Hopa, reaching for her shoulder and pulling her away from the animal. 'They mustn't find us.'

It seemed, however, that Apo Hopa's words had been uttered too late. The small band of soldiers had come to a halt. One of the riders was looking towards the trees as though something, a movement or a sound, had drawn his attention to that particular spot. Annabelle was attempting to tug the ragged material of her blouse free of the hand that gripped it, and, fearing her resistance would be sufficient to betray their position, Apo Hopa released her. She could only hope that the young American woman would heed her words and give the soldiers no cause to investigate this wooded stretch along the stream. Anxiously she watched the six uniformed riders, knowing that if they veered towards the trees they would surely be discovered. Alone, perhaps she could elude them, but she had to remain with Annabelle Goodwin, who wouldn't hide from those she was keen to accept as her rescuers.

Indeed, no sooner had she been released from Apo Hopa's grip than the senator's daughter took matters into her own hands. Disregarding the part Apo Hopa had played in freeing her from captivity, Annabelle was unable to regard her in any other light than as a person of those tribes from whom she was desperate to escape. So, while Apo Hopa's attention was fixed on the activity of the group of soldiers, Annabelle seized her opportunity. Quickly and silently she picked up a large stone and crashed it against Sky's head. While the Sioux was stunned and lying on the ground, she clambered into the saddle and rode the cavalry horse out from among the trees.

Struggling to her feet, touching her head where it had been opened by the hard rock, Apo Hopa watched as horse and rider raced away, aware that she could do nothing to prevent them reaching the military detail.

Major Shannon, alerted by a trooper's yell, brought his small command to a halt by raising his right arm high in the air. Even before the approaching rider had covered half the distance from the trees from which she'd emerged, her flying hair had betrayed her sex, and although there was little room for doubt, its fairness clearly identified her as Annabelle Goodwin. The popularity of the senator's pretty daughter during her short visit to Fort Hamilton had been widespread and her abduction a cause for much regret. Few had expected to see her again, so despite the dirt, injuries and expression of wide-eyed desperation, her appearance raised the spirits of the small group of soldiers.

When she reached them, she almost fell from the saddle. Exhausted by the trials of the previous days, overcome by the imminence of death and even the fear of her rescuers, her final strands of stamina had been driven out of her during that short, pell-mell ride from the tree-line. She clung on to her mount's mane as it came to a halt beside the other cavalry horses, and with eyes closed, had swayed in the saddle.

Now, fearing she would fall, Major Shannon jumped off his horse and helped her down. Her breathing was uneven, sometimes raggedy as though she'd forgotten how it was done. Sometimes she shook with sobs of panic as she struggled to get air into her body, and sometimes she drew in great gulps that seemed fit to burst her lungs. Major Shannon called for a canteen, soaked his own yellow neckerchief with some of its water and wiped it across her brow and cheeks to ease her consternation. Eventually, he let her drink a few drops from the canteen, and then she was ready to talk.

'We've been looking for you,' said Major Shannon. 'How did you get away?'

'Someone came for me,' she told him. 'A man with an Indian wife.'

'Wes Gray!'

'She called him Medicine Feather.'

Major Shannon nodded to let her know it was the same person. 'Why are you alone? Where are they now?'

'We heard shooting from the other side of the hill, where I was held captive. Medicine Feather went to investigate.'

'And the squaw?' This question was posed by Sergeant Watts, his aggressive tone startling Annabelle.

'Over there.' She pointed towards the trees.

Instantly, Sergeant Watts swung his horse around and headed in that direction. Major Shannon considered shouting an order for his return but refrained. The sergeant, he believed, considered himself subject only to orders issued by Captain Faraday and would pretend not to hear. Instead, he sent two of the troopers after him with orders to bring Apo Hopa back for questioning.

From her place among the trees, Apo Hopa watched the ministrations of the soldiers, and read Annabelle Goodwin's gestures as the American girl pointed first to the hills and then towards the woodland in which she was hidden. That they would come for her wasn't in doubt – indeed, already a rider was spurring in her direction, and by his bulk she knew him to be Sergeant Watts. For a moment the idea of stepping forwards to meet him crossed her mind – it was, after all, her intention to rejoin her people – but Wes had urged her to stay away from the soldiers. He didn't trust any of those who had destroyed her village, and indeed, she already had experience of the brutality of the man who was fast approaching. He'd beaten her without cause in front of her own house, and had kept her alive only to entrap her husband.

Even now, it occurred to her, Medicine Feather could be in danger. There was no reason to suppose that Sergeant Watts was the only soldier who had trailed them to this place. Perhaps the shooting beyond the hill was testimony to the fact that the camp of Wolf Necklace and the other braves had been found and was under attack. If so, no prisoners would be taken. Her husband, too, would be a target, but she had faith in his ability to survive. He would come back for her, so she must survive, too. She turned and ran.

The cluster of trees that lined the western bank of the stream stretched for less than half a mile. They comprised a surprising mixture of oak, beech and sycamore, most with stout trunks and boughs heavy with leaves that blocked the sun and created strange and confusing shadows, which benefited Apo Hopa in her efforts to escape the oncoming cavalryman.

Because Sergeants Watts alone was racing towards her, Apo Hopa's fear for her own safety was limited. Being able to move more rapidly between the close growing trees than even the best schooled horse, she believed she had the ability to escape her pursuer. She knew the art of concealment, could use trees and bushes to escape searching eyes, could remain so still as to be passed over unnoticed. It would be different if the whole detachment undertook a determined sweep of the woods. Six men scouring such a small area would eventually find her and drive her out of this timber refuge.

Beyond the woodland confines, even across the narrow stream, the sparse shrubbery offered little cover for a fugitive. As she darted among the trees, Apo Hopa scanned left and right for a suitable place to hide. Behind her the drumming of hoof beats slowed as the horse reached the tree-line. She had the small knife with which to defend herself, but that, she knew, was only useful at close quarters. There was only a slim chance that she would ever be able to use it.

'Come out,' yelled Sergeant Watts, 'show yourself.'

The sound barely reached Apo Hopa as intelligible words, but she stopped running, not to accede to his command but because a nearby split tree seemed to offer a suitable hiding place. It took only a few moments for her to realize its inadequacies. When she squeezed into the gap it soon became apparent that although she was well concealed she was also trapped if spotted by her hunter. In addition, she was almost cut off from all sound. Without her knowledge, Sergeant Watts could be at the other side of the tree. So cautiously, she left that place and moved silently among the trees. From behind came the sounds of snapping twigs, horse sounds, and the occasional shout or evil promise vented by Sergeant Watts. Apo Hopa moved on, then chose a chokeberry bush under which to lie. From that place she was able to better judge the mounted soldier's location. She couldn't see him, but by putting her ear to the ground she could tell in which direction he was moving, and if he was getting closer.

That was when she became aware that Sergeant Watts was not alone. Other riders had reached the woods and were moving cautiously among the trees.

Now the act of concealment was more difficult. Any movement that put her beyond the sight of one searcher might make her visible to another. Even her current position, although it provided a suitable point to watch for pursuit from the direction from which the nearest sounds of search emanated, was open to discovery from behind. She needed to move, to find a more secure hideaway, but until she knew how many men she needed to avoid and their current positions, she chose to stay under the bush, close to the ground.

Apo Hopa caught her first glimpse of Sergeant Watts as he ducked under the bough of an old oak, then halted to scan all around before nudging his horse forwards again. He was using only his legs and feet to guide his mount, as his hands were carrying his saddle carbine – and it was clear by the way he carried it that he was eager to use it. Gently, Apo Hopa rested her hand on the hilt of her knife. This time she was ready for him. If she was discovered, he wouldn't find it so easy to put hands on her again.

At one moment he was looking on the ground as though the possibility existed of finding footprints that would lead him to her, the next, he was trying to see around trees as though in the expectation of ambush. All the time he was muttering imprecations and threats in the hope that they would add to her fear if she could hear them.

To his right, an unseen trooper called his name.

'Have you got her?' Sergeant Watts wanted to

know, and wasn't disappointed with the negative answer he received. Wes Gray and his squaw would never get out of these hills alive, but there were things he could do to her before she died that would give him great pleasure. He didn't want the fort soldiers spoiling his plans. Still, he moved towards the voice, perhaps he could use a little help to chase her into the open.

With his back turned, Apo Hopa took the opportunity to move. Her intention was to double back, find a place of refuge in the part of the wood that Sergeant Watts had already passed through, and which was nearer the hills. But the very moment she emerged from under the bush coincided with the arrival of the trooper who was seeking Sergeant Watts. Seeing him, she was forced to seek the cover of the nearest tree, and from there move swiftly to put as much distance as possible between herself and the soldiers. She was heading towards the stream, beyond which there was little cover.

Although the trooper hadn't yelled an alarm, hadn't even pointed at the darting figure, his glance of surprise had been enough to inform the sergeant of the activity to his rear.

'Was it her?' he asked.

'Something moved,' was all the trooper said, but his answer was only directed at the sergeant's back, because already Watts was guiding his horse among the trees in pursuit.

Stopping once or twice to assess the situation, Apo

Hopa was conscious of the fact that the soldiers were close on her heels. The trees she used were able to offer a momentary refuge, but the need for haste deprived her of the opportunity to find anything more secure. There seemed to be little chance of escape when she broke from the trees and found herself at the edge of the stream. Behind her she could hear her hunters, and although she couldn't see them, she knew they couldn't be far behind. Her choices were limited. Crossing the stream would only lead to her capture, the horses would overtake her before she covered a hundred yards. If she turned back into the woods she ran the risk of running into one of the soldiers, and she had to assume that all six were hunting for her. Her attention was on the stream, but it wasn't deep enough to swim in, nor were there reeds or any kind of dense riverside vegetation to provide cover. But a glance over her shoulder revealed movement, so she had to act quickly.

Although there was little water in the stream, its banks were a couple of feet deep. Knife in hand, Apo Hopa dropped to her knees on the stream bed and, pressing herself close to the sandy bank, crawled unseen upstream. There was a kind of recess in the bank a short distance away into which she was able to tuck herself. If anyone rode into the water they would surely see her, but she had no other hiding place. She covered the knife with her arms. If she needed to use it she would do so.

Moments later she heard the riders arrive on the

bank. One of them didn't stop, but rode into the water, his gaze on the empty far landscape. 'Must have doubled back,' said Mickey Rafferty who, when he turned his horse, looked straight at Apo Hopa.

'I don't mean to let her get away,' said Sergeant Watts on the bank above her.

Mickey Rafferty nudged his horse forwards, and brought it right up to the place where the fugitive was hiding, then turned it side-on to the bank so that she had to press herself more deeply against the side of the recess. If anyone else came into the water Rafferty's horse would provide a shield behind which she would be unseen.

'Perhaps she showed herself deliberately,' suggested Rafferty. 'Led us in this direction but doubled back to make a run for the hills. Lots of places there where she could hide.'

Any response Sergeant Watts had to that observation wasn't delivered, because at that moment another trooper hailed them from the bank further downstream.

'Major Shannon's orders,' he shouted. 'We're pulling out. He's concerned about Miss Goodwin, wants to get her back to the fort before nightfall.'

'What about the squaw?' asked Sergeant Watts.

'He says Miss Goodwin is his priority. You're to abandon the search.'

'An order is an order,' said Mickey Rafferty, and waited for Sergeant Watts to lead the way out of the wood.

Sergeant Watts did so, at first reluctantly, but he knew that without assistance he could be riding around in circles without ever finding his prey – but his despair was short lived. He had two Shoshone scouts at his disposal, and they were better than a whole troop of cavalry. They'd found her once, they would do so again.

TEN

Wes Gray had put the bodies of the Sioux youths together and covered them with bushes, boughs and rocks to keep them safe from scavenging animals. It wasn't much of a funeral service, but under the circumstances he wasn't able to do better. The Shoshone weren't given the same consideration. The spare horses were chased away, but Wes didn't think that those that had been ridden by the Shoshone scouts would stray far. They were cavalry mounts and were trained to stay where their riders left them.

Trailing Apo Hopa's blanketed mount, Wes rode his dappled filly back down the hillside and across the flat meadowland to the stretch of timber along the waterside. When his wife ran forwards to greet him with the details of Annabelle's defection to the soldiers, he was swift to allay her misgivings. Whether or not he'd exaggerated the value that would be accredited to him for returning the senator's daughter to the fort, his wife's safety was more important to him.

Nor was he surprised by the information that Major Shannon's command had been enlarged. Ever since he'd encountered the Shoshone he'd deemed it probable that there were other soldiers in the area. It wasn't feasible that the scouts had come so far from Captain Faraday's column without his authority and someone to issue their orders. The fact that they were accompanied by only one soldier, and that that one was Sergeant Watts, was testament to Captain Faraday's intention: he was as eager to be rid of Wes Gray as the senator in Washington, and was prepared to overlook any act of violence or brutality in order to achieve it. Wes had no doubt that the sergeant had been chosen for his ruthlessness, and that he was a man who would not enjoy being thwarted. Although he was now deprived of the assistance of the Shoshone scouts, he was unlikely to cease his efforts if thoughts of revenge were on his mind.

Only the part Mickey Rafferty had played in keeping Apo Hopa out of the hands of the sergeant gave Wes any satisfaction. He was grateful for the trooper's intervention. Whatever debt the Irishman believed he owed was now fully paid.

The plaudits for getting Annabelle Goodwin back to Fort Hamilton could go to Major Shannon, although that officer, Wes thought, might also come under criticism for allowing Apo Hopa to elude him. In essence, they were now free to make the journey to the Red Cloud Agency, but Wes couldn't just ignore his responsibility to Caleb Dodge and the people he was leading to California. He had to get a message to the wagon master, let him know that he would rejoin the wagon train when Apo Hopa was safe. It was a job for Curly Clayport if he was sufficiently recovered from his injuries. So when they had allowed sufficient time for the Fort Hamilton-bound soldiers to be clear of Deer Creek, they set out in that direction also, but once across would stay due south towards the cabin on the V-shaped piece of land where the Mildwater Creek meets the South Platte River.

They hadn't yet reached Deer Creek when Apo Hopa pulled her horse to a halt. Above them, just below the crest, a lone figure mounted on a brown piebald sat as still as the hill itself. There were three feathers in his hair, two of which pointed to the sky and the third hung down towards his left shoulder. Apart from a deerskin breechclout he was naked, but held a buffalo skin shield in his left hand and a long lance in his right.

A smile touched the face of Apo Hopa. 'It is my brother,' she said, 'Throws-the-Dust.'

As though her words had carried to him, the Ogallalah warrior kicked his heels against the flanks of his pony and set a downhill course to join them. There was paint on his face, yellow lines on his cheeks, and red across his brow that wasn't fresh. He shouted as he approached, 'Ayee,' which was less a greeting for a favourite sister, more a proclamation, a boast, which Wes suspected was directed at him. He

ENEMIES OF MEDICINE FEATHER

and Throws-the-Dust had long been friends, but the lance had been raised shoulder high as though in preparation for throwing, and he was whirling his warhorse in circles, curbing its impatience to attack.

Wes raised his open hand, the sign of peace among all the tribes of the Plains. In addition to the paint on Throws-the-Dust's face, Wes saw that there was also a black handprint on his chest. This signified that he'd recently killed a man in a hand-to-hand fight. The Sioux warrior's eyes flared with wildness when he fixed them on Wes.

'Where are the people of my village?' he asked.

It was Apo Hopa who replied, telling her brother of the sudden attack and removal of the people. 'They are being taken to the place where Red Cloud's people live. Our father is with them and I will journey there to join him.'

'You, too, should go there,' Wes told him.

Throws-the-Dust jerked his head as though using it to deflect the American's words. Although Throws-the-Dust's demeanour had always emphasized his pride, even haughtiness, the gesture seemed now to mark it with arrogance and scorn. To Wes Gray's surprise, he caught a hint of enmity that had never before existed between them.

'The Lakota people do not move at the bidding of the *wasicun*,' he said. 'Now the long knives flee before us or they will all be dead like those who lie along the Greasy Grass.'

'There's been a battle?'

'Ay-ee!' he shouted, turning his pony in a circle once more as though it was a symbolic ritual. 'A great victory,' he announced. 'They fell into our camp as they did in the vision of Tatanka Yotanka and all were killed.'

Tatanka Yotanka was the Hunkpapa medicine man, Sitting Bull. Wes figured there'd been a large gathering of the tribes if Hunkpapa and Ogallalah had camped together. 'All killed!'

'They were fools to attack our village. Warriors from all the tribes of the Sioux were camped there, Cheyenne and Arapaho, too. They were too few to defeat us and they were led by the greatest fool of all. Yellow Hair wouldn't listen to our warnings when he was alive, now, in death, he can't hear our shouts of victory.'

'Custer. Custer is dead?'

Once again, Throws-the-Dust shouted his cry of jubilation. 'Ay-eee. Now the whites will be driven from the land of the Sioux. The sacred hills will be ours forever and the game and buffalo will multiply to fill the stomachs of all our children.'

Wes listened to his friend's words, repetitions of those same longings and unrealistic expectations he'd heard spoken around campfires and at war councils for twenty years. But rather than the Sioux gaining mastery of the territory, he knew that the killing of Custer would only hasten the end of their free-roaming days. Nothing that he knew of those leaders, however, led him to believe they were naïve.

ENEMIES OF MEDICINE FEATHER

They wouldn't have remained along the Greasy Grass, but that village would surely have been disbanded and another, more secret location sought. 'Where are the people of Crazy Horse and Sitting Bull now?' he asked.

Throws-the-Dust confirmed Wes's thoughts, but the village hadn't moved en masse. Finding another place that would support the needs of so many people and provide sufficient grazing for the huge horse herd could not be quickly achieved. So each tribe had gone in search of its own location.

'I have been sent to carry the news to the villages and to summon more braves to push the *wasicun* forever from the hunting grounds of the Sioux. The people must learn that the white soldiers now tremble at the names of Crazy Horse, Sitting Bull and Gall.'

'No villages remain to hear your voice, Throws-the-Dust,' Wes told him. 'Like the tepees of Red Knife, they are all destroyed, scattered to the winds, and the people herded to the land chosen by the chiefs in Washington.'

A passion was burning within Throws-the-Dust that Wes had never before witnessed, and though, momentarily, the burning light in his eyes dimmed as he listened to the scout's words, it was swiftly rekindled. It was apparent to Wes that words alone could not extinguish his Sioux brother's conviction. Perhaps Throws-the-Dust was reacting to the battle, but it seemed more probable to Wes that he was under the influence of some spiritual belief. Many warriors rode into battle convinced of their immunity to enemy weapons because of visions and omens. Perhaps a convincing Medicine Man had told the people that the death of Custer was a sign of the Great Spirit's pleasure and a promise of total victory.

'Soon, it will be the homes of the white men that are destroyed, and our people will walk free on the land.'

'You cannot win, Throws-the-Dust. The soldiers will come again, and this time there will be as many as leaves in a forest.'

'We are not afraid to die,' stated Throws-the-Dust.

Wes wanted to tell him that the death of all the fighting men of the nation would achieve nothing, that the days of freedom for all the surviving people of the Plains were finished. Their future lives would be spent on reservation land chosen by the politicians in Washington. But that was a kind of captivity against which his own spirit revolted, and he knew he had no arguments that would satisfy Throws-the-Dust.

It fell to his sister to try to persuade Throws-the-Dust to abandon his plans to rejoin Crazy Horse, and to go with her to the Red Cloud Agency. But even though her words were an echo of her husband's gloomy thoughts, a prediction that the free-roaming days of the Plains tribes were at an end and a new way of life must be embraced if the nations were to survive, she was still unable to hide her pride in her brother's achievements in battle. Killing their enemies was the role of the warriors, and the fading paint marks on his body told of his bravery and success in the recent fight. She rejoiced in her brother's pride. Consequently, her words lacked any power to convert him to reservation life.

There was little more to say. Wes stretched out his arm, the sign of peace as Throws-the-Dust prepared to depart, and was pleased when it was returned. Brother and sister exchanged words, then sat in silence for a moment as though each suspected that it would be the last time they saw each other. Then with a series of yips, such as he would have shouted when attacking a herd of buffalo, Throws-the-Dust turned his pony and set off to find the lodges of Crazy Horse's followers among the hills and valleys along the Yellowstone.

Wes and Apo Hopa continued their journey in silence, each occupied by thoughts that provided little happiness. Even so, instinctively, both were watchful of their surroundings. Although Sergeant Watts had ridden away with the soldiers from Fort Hamilton, there was no reason to suppose he was still with them. He'd be expecting the Shoshone scouts to report back to him. If Annabelle Goodwin had divulged that the gunfire had come from the place where she'd been held captive, then he might have gone over the hill to investigate.

As they approached the fording point at Deer

Creek they became aware of an approaching rider. Cautiously, they took refuge among some trees and waited for the other to appear. Wes drew his rifle from its saddle boot in anticipation that the rider was wearing a blue uniform and seeking to do them harm. The newcomer was moving slowly, like someone unsure of the territory or looking for tracks and signs. Wes and Apo Hopa remained still and watched as the lone rider in a familiar jacket and old slouch hat came into view. When Curly Clayport reached the water and checked his horse's progress, they rode forwards to greet him.

'What are you doing up in these hills?' Wes asked.

'Came looking for Sky. Thought she might need my help.'

'What made you think that?'

'I was heading for the cabin when I met up with Major Shannon and his men. They had the missing girl with them, were taking her back to the fort. She wasn't faring well, looked damn near ready to fall off her horse with exhaustion, but the major had a glint in his eye like a man who'd just won the last hand at a St Louis poker table. Reckon he could see more braid on his uniform for rescuing a senator's daughter.'

Wes didn't argue with his old friend's assessment of Major Shannon's expectations, nor did he appraise him of the officer's minor role in securing Annabelle Goodwin's freedom. 'Doesn't explain why you came up here looking for Apo Hopa.'

'Well, the major was anxious to get back to Fort Hamilton, but that big Irish trooper Rafferty hung back long enough to let me know that Sky was alone and in danger. He told me I'd find her upstream among some trees. His tone implied urgency, so here I am.'

'Was the sergeant still with the major and his men?' Wes wanted to know.

Curly slowly shook his head, an indication that he was giving the matter some thought before answering. 'No,' he drawled out, 'I didn't see a sergeant among the soldiers.'

'Not just any sergeant,' Wes told him, 'it was the one who came to the cabin and inflicted the injuries on you and Apo Hopa.'

Curly's expression darkened as memories of the beating he'd taken rose afresh in his mind. He shook his head again, this time more vigorously, certain of his answer. 'He wasn't with them,' he said.

'Then he must be somewhere in these hills, presumably seeking the Shoshone scouts he'd brought with him.'

Wes nudged his horse to create a bit of room between himself and Curly to enable him to replace his rifle in its scabbard, but before he could do so a shot rang out and a cry of shock and pain caused him to turn his head. Apo Hopa's eyes seemed so large that, momentarily, he was transfixed by them. Then her hands released the reins they had been holding and stretched out as though she was reaching for him, and her mouth moved as though she had words to tell him, but they never came. Blood spurted through the ragged hole in her dress and she fell to the ground.

ELEVEN

Shortly after rejoining Major Shannon and riding alongside that officer towards Deer Creek, Sergeant Wilbur Watts saw the sign he'd been seeking: two cuts in the bark of a tree forming an arrowhead, which marked the direction taken by Toshawa and Half Face. He wasn't surprised that they guided him uphill, because the girl had revealed that she'd been held in the valley beyond and had provided the additional information that it was gunfire from that direction that had caused Wes Gray to leave her and the squaw behind while he went to investigate.

He'd spared a look or two for Annabelle Goodwin, amused by her distress, sure that she was on the verge of fainting and falling from her mount. Her face, he believed, was whiter now than it had been when she'd first come galloping across towards them. She reminded him of a young soldier who'd lost his nerve the first time he'd come under fire. Without pity, Watts had watched the colour drain from the young fellow's face, then ordered him into an advanced position. The terrified youth hadn't gone two paces forwards before a bullet took off the top of his head. Watts had scoffed at the young man's demise. To his thinking, such recruits were worthless and shouldn't be sent into the West. That sentiment was also true of young women. If they couldn't stomach the rough ways of the frontier they should stay away.

He left Major Shannon's detail and began the climb into the hills. He had no reason to doubt the cause of the gunfire: the scouts had surprised the four young Sioux braves and slaughtered them. Perhaps by now they'd also killed Wes Gray, but he hoped he wasn't too late for that party. Still, if he was, there was always the squaw to go back to. If she thought she'd escaped she was in for a great shock. The Shoshone scouts would derive great pleasure from hunting her, but he would deal out the punishment.

The grass that had been flattened by the scouts' horses made their trail easy to follow. Before reaching the summit of the first hill they'd swung left, following a natural contour that took them around the hillside. There were hills all around, and Watts figured that he was at the beginning of high ground that stretched far to the north and west with numerous valleys that had probably never been marked on any map. He was pleased the Sioux hadn't gone deeper into the folds before making camp; as it was, without the Shoshone to guide him, it was unlikely he'd have been able to find his way out again.

Ahead, a long ridge stretched away, descending for perhaps a mile to the valley floor. But the tracks continued around the hillside, and Sergeant Watts stayed with them until he found a place where the Shoshone had dismounted and continued on foot. At this point he was still unable to see into the valley, but ahead he could see patches of flattened grass where, he supposed, Toshawa and Half Face had spied on the events below. He, too, dismounted, dropped the reins and made his way forwards.

The buzzards that flew up from a nearby bush took him by surprise. His hand reached for the revolver in his buttoned-down holster, but as he watched the birds fly away he knew it was his arrival that had disturbed them so he wasn't in any imminent danger. Even so, when he reached the bush, he peered around it cautiously. He'd anticipated seeing the body of one of the young Sioux braves, perhaps a guard caught unawares by one of the more experienced Shoshone scouts, but it took only a glimpse for that assumption to be driven from his mind. Although the face had been attacked and bore the marks of the razor sharp beaks of the scavenging birds, Sergeant Watts was still able to recognize Toshawa. This was because their main course had come from a more central point on the body. Toshawa's flimsy shirt was bloodied and shredded and the Shoshone's intestines had been dragged out and fought over by the greedy buzzards. Warm blood and scraps of flesh had been scattered all around, beaks and talons opening further the gap that had been created by the point of Wes Gray's knife.

Now, Sergeant Watts withdrew his pistol. His lips curled in a silent snarl as he recollected the girl's account of her captors. Not much more than boys, she had told Major Shannon, but that couldn't have been true. He could see Toshawa's knife lying a few yards away, evidence that he'd been involved in a knife fight, but that scout, he figured, was too experienced in such matters to fall foul of an untried youth. Eastern girls, he thought again, savagely, weren't even capable of providing an accurate report. They should stay at home.

Slowly he moved forwards to find a point from which he could look into the valley. Below, all seemed peaceful – nothing showed to indicate a gun battle had occurred. In the sky, however, the buzzards still circled, waiting, he supposed, to continue their feast. Still, alive or dead, Half Face had to be nearby, so he climbed on to his horse and began to descend gently and warily down the hillside.

He had almost reached the bottom when he saw the horses, two grazing peacefully in a fold at the foot of the hill that had kept them hidden from his sight. They lifted their heads, ears pricked as though they'd been awaiting his arrival and were now ready to follow. The sergeant was sure that they were the cavalry mounts that had been ridden by Toshawa and Half Face. Each had a saddle on its back, and he wouldn't have expected that of any horse belonging to the Sioux. He ignored them and rode on, because a quarter of a mile away a long ribbon stretched and fluttered in the breeze.

He passed a curious pile of rocks before he reached the maroon ribbon, but by that time he'd recognized its flagpole as a Sioux war lance, and had become suspicious of the untidy heap into which it had been planted. He reined to a halt but didn't dismount. An ugly grimace proclaimed that for Half Face death had not been easy. The gaping mouth and bulging eyes that had been his last living reactions as he was speared to the ground would be with him until the wind blew away his dust or the wild animals divided up his body.

Sergeant Watts had seen many corpses and sneered without pity at the apparent suffering of their final moments, but there was no laughter this time. Something had happened here that didn't fit the known facts. Toshawa's body had given him reason to doubt Annabelle Goodwin's description of her captors, but now his thoughts followed a different track. Perhaps the Sioux had been victorious against their tribal enemies and ridden away, but he wasn't convinced that the two Shoshone scouts would have attacked if the larger force had consisted of seasoned Sioux warriors. And the girl had reported much gunfire, yet neither Toshawa nor Half Face had been shot. He looked at the lance with its multiple decorations; the long maroon ribbon was of little interest to him, it was the scalps that held his interest. If Sioux warriors had killed Shoshone they would have taken their hair as trophies, but the scouts hadn't been scalped, which led him to only one conclusion.

'Medicine Feather,' he said, and in that moment he knew he must either seek him out alone or report a failed mission to Captain Faraday. Neither option appealed to him, although he didn't regard his reluctance to continue the search as a sign of fear, it was simply a fact that he'd been depending on the Shoshone to find the man for him. His own tracking skills were negligible, and even if he now chose to abandon the search for Wes Gray, he would have difficulty finding his way out of these hills to rejoin Captain Faraday's command.

Although he gave momentary consideration to rounding up the grazing horses which could be used in relay, he showed callous disregard for the bodies of his former scouts. They were left for the wild beasts, and he rode back around the hill and down to the place where he'd parted company with Major Shannon and his men. He figured that they were now a couple of hours ahead, but their tracks were clear. If he followed them they would surely guide him back to the trail the column had taken from Fort Hamilton. But he cast his eyes in the other direction, back to the distant line of trees where the squaw had hidden from him. He quickly dashed his initial thought that she might still be there and at his mercy if he went in search of her. Medicine Feather, he supposed, who must have quit the valley at the other side of the hill shortly before he, Sergeant Watts, had found Toshawa's body, would already be reunited with her. It would be foolish to ride into that plantation where death could be waiting for him behind any tree.

Further thought led him to the conclusion that the pair he was seeking wouldn't have lingered in that place. With Annabelle Goodwin already under military protection they no longer had a need to go to Fort Hamilton, so had probably fled to avoid the squaw being sent to the Red Cloud Agency. Their knowledge of this territory would make it impossible for him to find them, but he would be at their mercy if he continued the pursuit. He recalled Medicine Feather's threat to cut out his heart if he again harmed the squaw; perhaps chasing her into hiding gave him reason enough to carry it out. He spat on the ground with such emphasis that it seemed to solemnize his decision. He turned his horse again and set off in pursuit of the soldiers who were making their way to Fort Hamilton.

Like a good cavalryman, Sergeant Watts was conscious of the abilities of his mount. Although it was a strong horse, it had been carrying him since sunup and was deserving of an hour's rest. But there were few hours of daylight remaining, and to get clear of the hills before darkness fell depended upon him being able to see the trail left by the party ahead. So he maintained a steady canter, hoping that the regular rhythm of its stride would conserve the animal's energy while it ate away the miles that must be covered. Somewhere ahead he had to cross a stream; he would rest there awhile because that marked the end of the maze-like hill country and the route back to the column would be easy to find.

While he rode, however, he maintained vigilance. The prospect of encountering or being trailed by a vengeful Wes Gray was unwelcome, but he couldn't rid it from his mind. The day was warm, but there were beads of sweat on his brow and upper lip that weren't caused by the sun. Every now and then, when he thought he'd caught a glimpse of movement on a hillside or heard an indecipherable sound, he'd put spur to his horse, only to rein it back when he realized he'd merely been spooked by his own imagination. That was until he heard the unmistakable sound of a human voice carrying to him from the trail ahead. It was high-pitched, almost a scream: 'Yip! yip!'

Halting, he armed himself with his rifle, ears attuned for further sounds and his eyes scanning the land, which sloped away ahead limiting his vision. But the drumming sound that reached him came from a galloping horse, so he guided his own into the cover of some trees further up the hillside and waited.

A Sioux brave on a brown piebald appeared and passed within fifty yards of him. Rifle in hand,

Sergeant Watts had the opportunity to shoot at the warrior, but he held fire. Surprise had a part to play in his decision, he had not expected to see a feathered warrior with paint marks on his face, body and horse. However, he was quick to grasp the possibility that this warrior had been one of Annabelle Goodwin's captors and, if so, others could be in the vicinity. If he fired, the gunshot would advise them of his location. He wasn't a fool, he had no wish to die at the hands of hostile warriors. He considered the possibility that they had attacked Major Shannon's detail in order to recapture the girl. Perhaps, ahead, he would find evidence of an encounter. He waited ten minutes, and when no other sound arose to cause alarm, he continued more cautiously on his journey.

Shortly, as he began to descend through some trees, his horse threw its head in a manner that was indicative of a reaction to one of its senses – sight, sound or smell. Sergeant Watts believed it was the smell of water in its nostrils, because by now they must be close to the stream they needed to cross. Still wary of encountering more Sioux warriors, he kept his mount on a short rein as he moved slowly forwards. His caution was rewarded when voices reached him. With their two-hour lead, he ought not yet to have caught up with Major Shannon. If he had, then it was probably because they'd run into trouble with hostiles. With that in mind, and suspecting that they would be on guard against another attack, he moved forwards as quietly as possible.

At no time had it occurred to Sergeant Watts that the two people he'd been sent to kill were ahead of him on the trail. Although he knew that their home was on the Mildwater Creek, he hadn't given any consideration to the possibility that they would return to it. If they meant to keep the squaw off the reservation he would have expected them to make a run for the wild country where the army hadn't yet reached. So when he saw them paused at the side of the stream he almost uttered aloud an oath of victory. The fact that a third person was with them only gave him momentary pause. He recognized the older man, had smashed his fist into his face a couple of times before hitting him with stout stick he'd found lying in the yard outside their cabin. If he had to kill him too, then so be it. He raised his rifle, picked a spot on Wes Gray's back, and pulled the trigger.

Instinctively, as Apo Hopa's hands seemed to reach for him, Wes leant forwards in an effort to grasp them – but she was falling before he could reach her. Still, anxious to hold her, to give her his strength and protection, he dropped with her, hoping to catch her before she hit the ground. It was an action that saved his life. Not only did the next bullet pass harmlessly over his head, but he and Apo Hopa landed between the horses and were hidden from the gunman.

Denied a clear shot at either of his prime targets, Sergeant Watts hurriedly fired a bullet in Curly

Clayport's direction. If he'd paused a moment to steady his aim he would surely have been successful, because devoid of the agility of earlier years and further handicapped by the injuries he had already suffered at the hands of the soldier, Curly was slow in getting out of the saddle. But reacting to the reports of the rifle so close to its ears, Sergeant Watts' horse was fidgety, and its movements, coupled with his own hastiness, meant that that bullet, too, flew harmlessly across the creek.

Dismounted, Curly crept under his horse's belly into the triangle of safety created by the animals. He knelt beside his friends, could see that Apo Hopa's eyes had begun to take on that unseeing sheen that boded ill for her chances of survival. Wes, so often the provider when a cool head was required, seemed bemused in the current situation. He was muttering his wife's name as though trying gently to wake her from restful slumber, but at the same time using his left hand to press on her chest in an effort to hold back the blood she was losing. His rifle was gripped tightly in his right hand.

'If we're going to save her we can't let him keep us pinned down,' Curly said.

Those words had an instant affect on Wes. At that moment, saving Apo Hopa was all that mattered to him. She was still now, as though no longer breathing. Her eyes were closed and her parted lips were beginning to change colour. With his right hand he touched her brow, a gesture of tenderness that belied the expression of fury etched on to his face. He heard Curly say, 'I won't leave her,' before moving so suddenly and aggressively that Sergeant Watts was taken completely by surprise.

Pushing against the dapple's rump to open up the triangle of horseflesh, Wes came around its tail with his rifle spitting lead towards the trees where his foe was located. Eight times he fired, pulling the trigger, ejecting the shell, pulling the trigger, with such rapidity and accuracy that the soldier failed to return fire.

Bullets whined around the sergeant, some smacked against tree trunks and others sent twigs flying near his head. Among the rounds fired at him one seared a line along his right arm from wrist to elbow, causing him to drop his rifle. He could see the buckskin-clad plainsman advancing, almost running up the hillside to reach him. Yanking at the reins, he turned his horse and set it at a gallop along the trail that had brought him to that place. Two more bullets hurried him along, but the trees prevented any chance of being hit.

When Wes returned to the others, Curly was using his neckerchief as a pad to soak up the blood that Apo Hopa was losing. He spoke only two words: 'Get him,' he told Wes.

Wes was glad to have the dappled filly under him. In addition to being responsive to his commands, it was a game animal, one that would run until its heart burst if that was necessary. Wes had followed Sergeant Watts' line through the trees until he reached the meadowland, with low hummocks to his left and the stream that led down to Deer Creek on his right. The soldier was not much more than a quarter of a mile ahead, watchful, throwing looks over his shoulder, attempting to judge the distance between them until he considered that his pursuer was within pistol distance. He fired twice without success.

Wes drew closer but didn't return fire: he didn't want Sergeant Watts to die by the gun. When the soldier looked back, Wes steered the dapple to the right, as though he meant to cut him off where the water course formed a loop ahead. But when the other returned his attention to get the best effort from his own horse, Wes switched the dapple to the right and used the low humps to hide behind. When he looked back again, Sergeant Watts was confused by the disappearance of the scout.

By now, Wes had almost drawn level with his prey. The picture in his mind was of Apo Hopa bleeding to death as she lay on the ground. Sergeant Watts deserved no mercy. At the appropriate moment, when the soldier was searching for sight of him along the river, he came over the low mound and rode the dappled filly straight at the other's horse. It was a tactic used in battle by the Sioux: an unhorsed enemy was a dead enemy.

The horses collided and Sergeant Watts lost his

grip on another gun. His horse went down, spilling him out of the saddle so that he struck the ground heavily before rolling over the grass. The dapple, too, stumbled, but although its front knees buckled it was able to find its feet and stay upright. This was partly due to Wes jumping out of the saddle on impact so that it could fend for itself.

Now Wes was scampering over the turf in pursuit of his foe, moving almost on all fours, touching the ground with hands and feet as though he was a big cat balancing itself before pouncing. Sergeant Watts was trying to reach the pistol that had been flung from his hand, but it was a forlorn effort. Wes acted swiftly, gave the soldier no chance to escape. He pinned him to the ground, stunned him with a blow from the bone handle of his knife before pulling tight his hair then slicing off the top of his head. He held the scalp high so that the blood dripped on to its owner's agony-twisted face.

'I am Medicine Feather. Brother of the Arapaho and friend of the Sioux,' Wes intoned. The words 'their enemies are my enemies,' remained unspoken. This time it was personal. 'And now,' he said, 'your heart.'

EPILOGUE

Even before the death of Sergeant Watts, Wes Gray's feud with Jeremiah Goodwin was at an end. On a visit to a town in Indiana, the senator had fallen victim to an outbreak of cholera, and neither political influence nor wealth of dubious provenance were able to save him. Whatever reaction he would have had to Medicine Feather's part in the restitution of his daughter to the care of the military no longer mattered; indeed, he died never knowing that she had been a captive of hostile Sioux.

News of her father's death awaited Annabelle Goodwin at Fort Hamilton, providing her with a suitable reason for leaving the following day, sparing her everything but the most cursory enquiries into her treatment at the hands of her captors. In fact, she was more remembered at that place for the vitriolic comments she delivered with regard to her rescuers, implying that Wes and Apo Hopa were no more civilized than her captors.

ENEMIES OF MEDICINE FEATHER

On her return to Washington, she lived for a while with her elder sister, whose husband was the lawyer Mark Owenfield. He had been their father's co-conspirator in the attempt to instigate a war with the Sioux in order to grab the rights to the gold in the Black Hills, but without the backing of Jeremiah Goodwin, his prominence in Washington was soon to fall away. He devoted the rest of his life to expanding his law firm. He had never met Wes Gray and had no desire to do so. He was content to stay in the cities of the east, and hoped that the other remained on the wide-open western plains.

Captain Faraday, too, upon receiving news of the senator's death, set aside further thoughts of conflict with Wes Gray. The senator's death not only put an end to the speculation of further rapid advancement, but also to the expectation of impunity for his actions. Although he never received confirmation of the deaths of Sergeant Watts, Toshawa and Half Face, he never doubted that they'd been slain by the plainsman he'd despatched them to kill. Until he reached the Red Cloud Agency, and for several days after, he expected to be confronted by a vengeance-seeking Wes Gray. But such a meeting never materialized, and in the wake of the Battle at the Little Bighorn, he and his men were ordered to join General Crook's army who were in the field to force the final submission of the tribesmen. Weeks later he was killed during one of the skirmishes leading up to the surrender of American Horse at Slim Buttes.

Although she teetered between life and death for several days, Apo Hopa survived. The miracle was partly achieved by Curly's early determination to prevent significant blood loss, but mainly due to the expertise of the surgeon from Fort Hamilton. Clandestinely, setting aside his military duty in favour of his Hippocratic oath, Doctor Bart James tended to her without reporting the matter to his superior officer. If aware of Sky's presence in the cabin by the Mildwater Creek, Colonel Finch would have been compelled to send her north to rejoin her people. In the surgeon's opinion, such a journey would nullify his efforts, and Sky would be dead before she reached the Red Cloud Agency. But he had a second reason for refusing to recognize that the wounded woman was classified as hostile by the army, and that was friendship and respect for her husband. Wes Gray had tried ceaselessly to foster understanding between red men and white, and in the doctor's opinion, that made him worthy of special consideration, and his wife deserving of his aid and protection.

But Apo Hopa was severely weakened by her injury and her recovery was slow, so although it remained her intention eventually to rejoin her people, Wes refused to let her travel until the harsh winter was over. By that time, Crazy Horse had been killed after surrendering at Fort Robinson, Sitting Bull had led his families across the border to try to find peace in Canada, and Red Knife's people had been moved to the Cheyenne River Reservation on the banks of the great Missouri. So it was to that place that Wes took his wife in the warmer months of 1877, and there she became a teacher to the young, interpreter and adviser to the councilmen, and recorder of the memories of the old so that the history and crafts of the Lakota people were not lost forever.

For a while, her husband continued to act as guide for the long trains of wagons that made the westward journey, but those days, too, were coming to an end. The railroads that stretched across the continent not only reduced the journey from months to days, but carried the people in greater comfort. But Wes Gray wasn't yet ready to settle on that V-shaped piece of land where the Mildwater Creek meets the South Platte River. He scouted for the army, he scouted for railway companies, he even acted as guide for private parties who wanted to hunt and witness the vastness of the untamed West – but he never forgot the debt he owed the people who no longer roamed that land, the people who had fed and sheltered him in his youth, and shown him how to survive in a wild, sometimes savage environment. He was Medicine Feather, brother of the Arapaho, friend of the Sioux, and even in defeat, their fights remained his fights and their enemies were his enemies.